the Cheetah Girls

Cuchifrita, Ballerina

Deborah Gregory

JUMP AT THE SUN

HYPERION PAPERBACKS FOR CHILDREN

NEW YORK

Printed in the United States of America

First Edition

1 3 5 7 9 10 8 6 4 2

This book is set in 12-point Palatino.

ISBN 0-7868-1476-4

Library of Congress Catalog Card Number on file.

Visit www.cheetahgirls.com

Fashion credits: Photography by Charlie Pizzarello. Models: Sabrina Millen, Sonya Millen, Imani Parks, Brandi Stewart, and Davida Williams. Apparel: Betsey Johnson, P. Fields, Nicole Miller, Sox Trot, Agatha Paris. Hair by Julie McIntosh. Makeup by Kathleen Herch and Tasha Vila. Fashion styling by Nole Marin.

For Amanda Barber,
my old school friend,
who's got the slander—
'cuz what's good for the goose
is good for the gander.
Quack, quack!

The Cheetah Girls Credo

To earn my spots and rightful place in the world, I solemnly swear to honor and uphold the Cheetah Girls oath:

- Cheetah Girls don't litter, they glitter. I will help my family, friends, and other Cheetah Girls whenever they need my love, support, or a *really* big hug.

- All Cheetah Girls are created equal, but we are not alike. We come in different sizes, shapes, and colors, and hail from different cultures. I will not judge others by the color of their spots, but by their character.

- A true Cheetah Girl doesn't spend more time doing her hair than her homework. Hair extensions may be career extensions, but talent and skills will pay my bills.

- True Cheetah Girls *can* achieve without a weave—or a wiggle, jiggle, or a giggle. I promise to rely (mostly) on my brains, heart, and courage to reach my cheetah-licious potential!

- A brave Cheetah Girl isn't afraid to admit when she's scared. I promise to get on my knees and summon the growl power of the Cheetah Girls who came before me—including my mom, grandmoms, and the Supremes—and ask them to help me be strong.

- All Cheetah Girls make mistakes. I promise to admit when I'm wrong and will work to make it right. I'll also say I'm sorry, even when I don't want to.

- Grown-ups are not always right, but they are bigger, older, and louder. I will treat my teachers, parents, and people of authority with respect—and expect them to do the same!

- True Cheetah Girls don't run with wolves or hang with hyenas. True Cheetahs pick much better friends. I will not try to get other people's approval by acting like a copycat.

- To become the Cheetah Girl that only *I* can be, I promise not to follow anyone else's dreams but my own. No matter how much I quiver, shake, shiver, and quake!

- Cheetah Girls were born for adventure. I promise to learn a language other than my own and travel around the world to meet my fellow Cheetah Girls.

Chapter 1

Bubbles is plopped in the seat next to mine on the plane—and she is sleeping with her cheetah jacket covering her head, which makes her look like one of those blob creatures from the Wack Lagoon. I think she's doing it because she doesn't want to talk to me. Although she hasn't said it (yet), I know Bubbles thinks the whole drama that went down in Houston is my fault. *La culpa mía.* Well, I'm not going to feel guilty! I stick one of my purple glitter star stickers on my bubble gum pink pants. Ooo, that looks *tan coolio!*

Feeling defiant doesn't get me out of the Dumpster, though. It's a sad Sunday, because the Cheetah Girls—that's Galleria "Bubbles"

The Cheetah Girls

Garibaldi, Dorinda "Do' Re Mi" Rogers, the twins (Aquanette and Anginette Walker), and, of course, me—Chanel "Chuchie" Simmons—are flying back to the Big Apple and going back to school. Our little gobblefest in Houston is definitely over. *Terminado.* I should be grateful that the Cheetah Girls got to spend Thanksgiving in the twins' hometown—even if it turned into *una tragedia.*

Actually, it was more like an episode on the Spanish soap opera *Oh, No, Loco!* See, the Cheetah Girls performed in the Miss Sassy-sparilla Contest at the Okie-Dokie Corral. Best of all, we won first place, because we sang this coolio song—"It's Raining Benjamins"—that I, Chanel Coco Cristalle Duarte Rodríguez Domingo Simmons, helped write. (I've decided if we ever publish a Cheetah Girls song to-gether, I'm going use my whole name on the credit. Hee, hee—Dominican stylin'.)

Anyway, it was obvious the Cheetah Girls deserved to win the contest, because we had our lyrics and choreography down. Everyone could tell, because at the end of the song, when we threw the fake Benjamins at the audience, they clapped loud enough to chase away a herd of buffalo.

Cuchifrita, Ballerina

After we collected our Miss Sassy trophy, though, our luck went south. One of the losing groups, CMG—the Cash Money Girls—got bitten by the green-eyed monster, and decided to run us out of town. They went around telling anybody who would listen that the Cheetah Girls stole the lyrics from *their* song "Benjamin Fever"—and even stole their routine bite for bite!

Well, all right, I did use a *couple* of words from "Benjamin Fever" for our song "It's Raining Benjamins." But how was I supposed to know you're not supposed to do that? When we called *Madrina* (my godmother and Bubbles's mom) in New York, she told us that we had perpetrated "copyright infringement." And okay, we did throw fake Benjies at the audience, just like CMG does. But I don't care what anybody says—our song was better than theirs, *está bien?*

Sticking more stickers on my pants, I let out a deep sigh. I guess the Cash Money Girls had reason to be jealous. See, we had performed on a bill with them once before—at the Tinkerbell Lounge in West Hollywood, for a New Talent Showcase sponsored by Def Duck Records.

(Yes, the same label that has Kahlua Alexander.) We got a lot of attention after the showcase, so maybe CMG thought the record company liked us better than them. Little do they know we're still sitting around waiting for a record deal, and to get into the studio with Def Duck producer Mouse Almighty.

I sink back into my seat, and try to cover my face with the little airline pillow, but it falls into my lap. Maybe I should try to write another song? No, I don't think Bubbles would like that. Without even realizing it, I start humming the chorus to the song that caused all the drama:

> "It's raining Benjamins for a change
>   and some coins.
> It's raining Benjamins . . . again!"

I just can't get that song out of my head, but I guess I'd better not let it fly out of my *boca grande*, because the Cheetah Girls promised CMG we would never sing "It's Raining Benjamins" again in public. I stick some more glitter star stickers on my pants legs, and before I know it, they look like the Hollywood Walk of Fame on Hollywood Boulevard. Well, we sure aren't strolling on the Walk of Fame right now!

I can't believe Bubbles let the Cash Money Girls bully us around like that. She even offered to give them our Miss Sassy trophy! *We* won it, not them! Luckily, CMG said, "No, thanks."

The truth is, I wish *I* could take home the Miss Sassy trophy. I'd like to show it to Mom, so she can see that the Cheetah Girls are the best singing group in the jiggy jungle. But Bubbles decided that the twins should keep it. After all, they're the reason we got to spend Thanksgiving in Happenin' Houston in the first place.

"Miss, could you please put your bags under your seat?" the flight attendant says to Aqua, snapping me out of my Houston memories.

"We don't put our purses on the floor, ma'am, 'cuz it's bad luck," Aqua explains earnestly. "You won't have any money left if you do that." She gives the flight attendant a look like she should understand. "You know, it's a southern thing."

I don't think the lady understands, because she just says, "Miss, you're gonna have to put your bags underneath the seat or in the over-head compartments."

"We'll do that, then," Angie says quietly. She waits until the lady walks away, then hides her purse under her blanket.

Even though I don't believe in their superstitions (only mine!), I can't blame the twins. It seems like they have a lot of rules in airplanes. For example, you can't polish your nails. You can't keep your belongings in your lap. You can't let animals sit in an airline seat, even though the twins paid seventy-five duckets for a seat for their guinea pigs, Porgy and Bess, so they could take them along. Seventy-five duckets! I'd buy twenty pairs of cheetah anklets from Oophelia's catalog before I parted with those kind of duckets for two furry creatures that chomp on carrots.

Don't get me wrong, I love pets. I even bought my little brother, Pucci, a cute little African pygmy hedgehog for his birthday—Mr. Cuckoo. "I hope Pucci has been taking good care of Mr. Cuckoo while I've been away in Houston," I say to the twins. Pucci's been staying with our *abuela*—our grandma—over Thanksgiving.

"I'm sure he's okay," Aqua chuckles back.

"You never know," I counter. Thinking about

Mom, I start nervously smoothing out my hair again. She's back now, from her trip to Paris with her boyfriend, Mr. Tycoon.

I feel flutters in my stomach, and a pang—*un poco dolor*—in my chest. I wish I had a nice family, like the twins. All my mother and I do is fight, and my brother Pucci only speaks to me when he feels like it. Of course, now he's being nice to me because I bought him Mr. Cuckoo.

I wonder if Daddy and his girlfriend, Princess Pamela, are back from Transylvania, Romania. That's where they went for Thanksgiving, so she could be with her family. I'll bet if I lived with them, Mom would miss me. Then she'd be sorry she gave me such a hard time. . . .

"I wonder if Pucci will let me take Mr. Cuckoo to the annual Blessing of the Insects and Their Four-Legged Friends at St. John's tonight," I say to Angie. "Probably not, but I'm going to take him anyway. Do you want to bring Porgy and Bess?"

"No, we have to go straight to our church with Daddy," Angie explains.

Maybe Bubbles will bring her dog, Toto, I think. I decide I'll ask her later, when she wakes up. Then I look around, and see that the lady sitting across the aisle is smiling at me.

"Howdy do," the lady says in a southern twang, which I'm used to now after spending a week in Houston.

"Hi," I say back, smiling.

"Y'all ain't from *Youston*, are you?"

"No, we're from New York," I say beaming, then add, "we're singers."

"Is that right?" the lady says excitedly. "Do you sing rip-rap?"

I look at Dorinda for help, but she is lost in her book, so I shrug my shoulders and ask politely, "Do you mean hip-hop?"

"Why, yes—isn't that the same thing?" the lady asks, amused at her own cuckooness, I guess.

"Um, yeah," I say, trying to be nice, "but not exactly. We mix all kinds of music and vibes together."

"Oh," the lady says. "Well, variety is the spice of life."

"We must be very spicy, then, because we mix a lot of music!"

The nice lady sees me eyeing the crumpled newspaper resting on her lap. "Would you like to see the paper?" she asks me. I nod yes, and she hands it to me.

"Ooo, Krusher's new album is out!" I coo to no one in particular, as I gape at the full-page advertisement for my favorite singer in the whole world. His eyes look so dreamy . . . like he's smiling right at me!

Dorinda takes her nose out of her book and peers over my shoulder.

"I think you have *un coco* on Krusher!" I tease Dorinda.

"I think he's cute, but I'm not mackin' him like you are," Dorinda says, throwing me a sly look.

"What happened? I'm gonna write him a letter," I say, like I have made a very big decision in my life, *mi vida loca*. Suddenly, I feel a sting in my chest, remembering the 1-900-KRUSHER contest that I entered. How could I have lost that? The deejay lady who won the stupid contest couldn't possibly feel the same way I feel about him.

"How old is he?" Dorinda asks, yawning.

"Nineteen," I say dreamily, touching his picture.

Dorinda gives me a funny look. "You really are goo-goo ga-ga for him!"

I get so embarrassed that I flip the page quickly. "You'll see," I say firmly. "What if we get to perform with him—I mean after we become famous, *está bien*?"

"We don't even have a record deal yet," Dorinda reminds me, sighing heavily and spoiling my *gran fantasía*.

"Maybe Def Duck records forgot about us," I say sadly.

"I hear that," Dorinda says matter-of-factly, but I can tell she feels sad, too.

My heart flutters even more when I turn the next page of the newspaper. It's a full-page ad for the American Ballet Theatre. A beautiful girl who looks a little older than me is pictured in a ballerina tutu, standing on her tippy-toes in pointe shoes with her arms outstretched over head. REACH FOR THE STARS! is sprawled across the picture in big letters. Underneath it says, "Auditions for the Junior Corps Division begin soon. Deadline for applications, November 24."

That's three days ago. This paper must be a week old!

I shoot a quick glance at Dorinda, to see if she notices how excited I am. Luckily, she's too busy staring at the picture in the ad to notice.

Cuchifrita, Ballerina

My heart is pounding like a jackhammer—I didn't realize the auditions were coming up so soon! See, about a month ago, I secretly sent in my application—and I've been waiting to hear from them ever since, practicing hard in case I got an audition. Now I realize that the first thing I have to do after school tomorrow is find out if I got an audition for the Junior Corps!

"Can you do that?" Dorinda asks chuckling.

"What happened?" I ask absentmindedly. Then I realize Dorinda is asking about the exquisite ballet pose in the picture. *"Sí, mamacita,"* I say defensively.

Dorinda giggles, because I fell in the twins' bedroom in Houston while trying to do a *battement tendu jeté* to the side, then leap across the room. I sprained my ankle, and it still hurts.

"The area rug in the twins' bedroom was slippery—that's all!" I complain.

"Is your ankle okay?" Dorinda asks gingerly.

"There's nothing wrong with my ankle," I shoot back. "It was just a little sprain. It's okay, *está bien?"* I stare adoringly at the ballerina in the picture, who is obviously playing the part

11

of Princess Aurora in "Sleeping Beauty"—my favorite classical ballet. Mom took me to see it when I was little. In my fantasies, I sometimes pretend that I am Princess Aurora.

"How long did you and Bubbles take ballet classes?" Dorinda asks, nudging me out of my daydream.

"Lemme see—we started when we were six or seven, then stopped in the sixth grade—no, it was the year Bubbles won the intermediate spelling contest . . . um, the second semester in seventh grade. I think that spelling contest went to her head."

"Well, you know how Bubbles likes the lyrical flow," Dorinda chuckles, like I should stop complaining. "Why didn't you keep doing it though—even after Bubbles stopped?"

I look at Dorinda like she is cuckoo. She knows that Bubbles and I are like sisters. Whatever Bubbles does, I do. That's just the way it is, ever since I can remember.

But now I'm beginning to wonder. I miss ballet, and this may be my last chance to prove I can do it—even if Mom thinks I can't. I can hear her now: "Chanel, your butt sticks out too much to be a ballet dancer!"

Cuchifrita, Ballerina

"I don't know, Dorinda—Bubbles didn't want to do it anymore, and I didn't want to do it by myself," I respond.

"I wish *I* could do it," Dorinda says wistfully.

Suddenly, I feel bad for whining. Dorinda never even had the chance to take ballet lessons, because she lives in a foster home, and they don't have any money. She probably could've danced circles around all the snobby girls that were in our class.

Now I know why Dorinda tried out for Mo' Money Monique's tour without telling us: *she wanted to see if she could do it.* Maybe I could do *this* without telling anybody, too. . . .

"Did you really want to go on tour with Mo' Money Monique?" I tease Dorinda. I know how badly she feels for trying out without telling us a little bo-peep about it.

"I guess not. I just wanted to make my teacher happy—she wanted me to do it," Dorinda says, trying to justify her actions.

Suddenly I hear the words come out of my mouth. "I'm going to try to get into the Junior Ballet Corps."

"Word?" Dorinda asks, surprised.

"*Sí, mamacita*—this may be my 'last chance,

last dance,' and I'm going to do it," I say, convincing myself. "You'll see."

The nice lady is looking over at us. "You seem to be really enjoying that newspaper. Why don't you keep it?"

"Really?" I ask.

"Of course," she says, waving her hand.

I look one last time at the picture of the ballerina, then fold it up carefully. I put it into my cheetah backpack, like it's a wish I have to put in Aladdin's lamp. In some ways, it is—I *have* to convince Mom to let me spread my wings again!

Chapter 2

As soon as I put my key in the front door, I start feeling nervous again. *Ay, Dios*, please don't let Mom pick a fight with me!

I've made up my mind that I'm going to tell Mom that I'm trying to get into the American Ballet Theatre's Junior Corps division. I know Mom is not feeling me these days, *está bien*, and part of it is my fault. *Tengo la culpa.* See, I got the *baboso* idea to charge up her credit card after she let me use it to buy me a new outfit. You can bet Mom is never gonna let me forget about that *catástrofe*. She will probably be telling my grandchildren the story when she's old and in a rocking chair! *Qué horrible!*

Maybe Mom will be happy for a change, now

that she got to spend a whole week in Paris with Mr. Tycoon. He is her new boyfriend, and she seems to be pretty cuckoo about him—even though he never looks me straight in the eye, or asks me anything about myself. I don't think the tycoon approves of my being in a singing group. Well, neither does Mom—so I guess they are perfect for each other!

Suddenly, I hear this screeching noise— *Whhrrrr, whrrrr, whrrrr*—coming in my direction from down the hallway. Just as I'm looking up, not only do I almost get my head sawed off by a fast-moving blur, but I trip and fall on my butt, letting out an involuntary scream. "Aaayeee!"

"So how was your trip, *loco* Coco?" Pucci giggles, making his way back toward me on this— scooter? Pucci likes to call me by my middle name—Coco—so he can prefix it with *loco*— crazy. He thinks he's funny. I'll show him.

"*Baboso*," I wince, eyeing the shiny silver scooter with the big purple Flammerstein and Schwimmer logo on its deck. That store is really expensive—that scooter had to cost at least $100! "Where did you get this?" I ask Pucci, grabbing his wrist.

Cuchifrita, Ballerina

"None of your business!" he smirks back, then wiggles his way out of my grip and makes a mad dash back down the hallway.

"Pucci!" I hear Mom's muffled voice yelling from the den. "I told you not to ride that thing in the house, *está bien?*"

Pucci scoots by like a *loco* Road Runner, then comes back down the hallway again.

"You heard *Mamí—párate!*" I hiss at Pucci until he finally stops.

"Why'd you have to come home?" he asks, scowling at me.

I ignore my pain-in-the-poot-butt brother. "Who got you that thing?" I demand.

Seeing me eye his new prized possession, Pucci huffs, "*Mamí* got it for me in Paris."

"*Por qué?*" I ask astounded. "It's not your birthday!"

"'Cuz I *wanted* one!" Pucci shoots back, grinning like the Cheshire cat—large and in charge.

That is so unfair! I say to myself. Mom would never buy me anything "just cause I wanted it." "Is Daddy back?" I ask Pucci, feeling the need to complain to somebody about Mom.

"Yup—he called me."

"Where?"

"At Abuela's house," Pucci snaps, like I'm stupid. "Daddy met Dracula—and he brought back his teeth." Snorting like Mr. Piggy, Pucci scurries away.

"He did not. And get off that thing!" I yell. Pucci is always telling fib-eronis. But who knows, maybe Daddy did meet some of Dracula's relatives in Transylvania! See, his girlfriend, Princess Pamela, is almost like royalty in her native land. She comes from a long line of Gypsy pyschics—and they are treated with respect in Romania—not like here.

I grab the newspaper out of my suitcase, and walk into the den. If I'm going to have a fight with Mom, it might as well be over something really important.

Anyway, I need to get this handled right away, because the auditions are coming up really soon. On the way into the den, I'm thinking, Mom can't say no. If she doesn't like me singing with the Cheetah Girls, why can't I join a ballet group? She wanted me to be a ballerina—and I stopped because Bubbles got tired of it. She should be happy that I want to do it again.

Ay, Dios mío! I gasp when I see Mom. What has she got on her *face*? I know that she does her beauty mask every Sunday afternoon, but this isn't like her yucky yellow mask—it's a lot scarier! It's a white plastic thing that kinda looks like a hockey mask, but creepier—and it's vibrating! I try not to stare, but her whole face is covered—except for the two holes for her eyes, the two dots for her nose, and the round hole for her mouth. Usually, when she does her mask ritual, she looks like the Mummy—but now she more resembles Hannibal the Cannibal in that scary movie we saw, *Silence of the Lambchops*, or whatever it's called.

Mom is sitting on the couch, flipping the pages of *Hola!* magazine. She looks up at me, her brown eyes like two beads peering out of the holes. Suddenly I feel too nervous to ask—because I can't even look at her!

"Don't stand there staring at me," Mom moans in a muffled voice. "This is a new skin-tightening mask. I got it in *Parrris*, at Maison Bouche—the most prestigious skin care *insti-toot in Parrrris*," Mom says, stretching out the rrr's. Wow, I think—her phony French accent has gotten better.

Wait a minute—how do I know this is my mother? Maybe this hockey face is really a clone, because Mr. Tycoon got rid of Mom!

"What's that noise coming from it?" I ask gingerly, backing up against the wall in case she tries to attack me or something.

"It vibrates to get the circulation going in the skin," Mom moans, like she wants me to stop bothering her. Now I'm sure the spooky hockey lady is Mom, and not a clone, because she is annoyed with me as usual. Defeated, I rest the weight of my body against the bookcase.

"Thank you for letting me go to Houston. We had a really good time," I say, telling *una poca mentira*—a little fib-eroni—so she'll be in a better mood. I'm not going to let her know what really happened.

"That's nice," she says, no longer looking at me, but engrossed in the pages of the magazine again. Mom is writing a book—*It's Raining Tycoons*—about women who date oil tycoons from Arabia. She is constantly doing research now, trying to find candidates—even though the book company told her she has to get a ghost writer or they won't publish it, because her writing isn't that good.

"We ate fried alligator sandwiches in Houston," I say, giggling.

"Eeuw—that sounds disgusting!" Pucci blurts out, sticking his big head into the den. He's so nosy, he gets on my nerves! I throw him a quick scowl and squint my eyes at him. "Too bad the alligator didn't bite you!" he snaps at me.

"Shut up, Pucci," I snap back, because I can't resist.

"*Mamí*, can I go to the park now?" Pucci asks. I should have known he was angling for something from Mom—he sure didn't come in here to see me!

"Did you clean your room?" Mom asks him.

"Yeah," Pucci says, rubbing his head.

"I don't want you going to the park by yourself."

"Moham is coming with me," Pucci protests.

"I don't want you two going any farther than the park on Thompson Street, *tú entiendes?*" Mom says, but I know she's really telling him, "You two had better not go uptown on those scooters."

"Okay," Pucci says, like he's kinda disappointed.

The doorbell rings and nobody moves. "Excuse me," Mom says, looking at us like we're *loco*. "It's the butler's night off—go answer the door!"

Pucci runs to the door, and I hear him talking to Moham. Then the two of them come into the den.

"You told Moham he could pick you up without checking with me first?" Mom asks, in that muffled, facial mask voice. It sounds like she's wearing a muzzle!

"He's just coming over. I didn't tell him I was going," Pucci protests.

Moham stands very politely in the doorway, waiting. He is so nice, I don't understand how Pucci and he can be friends.

Mom is not very happy about Moham being in the den. She is staring at his muddy sneakers.

"Hello, Mrs. Simmons," he says, staring warily at her fright mask.

"Hello, Moham."

"I'll . . . see you later," Moham says, scurrying out of the room followed by Pucci.

"I'm taking Mr. Cuckoo Cougar to the Blessing of the Insects and Their Four-Legged Friends," I call after Pucci.

"I don't want you taking him anywhere!" Pucci yells, turning around and glaring at me.

"You two stop it!" Mom shouts, as loud as she can with her hockey mask over her face.

"I want Mr. Cuckoo to be *blessed*!" I hiss.

"Pucci, let her take him to church!" Mom commands.

"Awright, but nothing better happen to him," Pucci says, shooting me a dirty look.

Moham smiles serenely, then asks curiously, "Where is it?"

"Saint John the Divine," I reply.

"Maybe I should bring my turtle," he chuckles.

"Don't laugh—there are people there with fishbowls, too!" I exclaim.

"We're not going there," Pucci mutters to Moham.

"Don't worry," Moham tells him. "We're Muslim—my mother wouldn't approve anyway." Moham drags his scooter out the front door, and Pucci is right behind him.

I go back into the den, to push my ballet scheme with Mom. I start by chatting away about Houston, to get her in a better mood.

"You should have seen the restaurant Mrs. Walker took us to," I say cheerfully. Mom loves five-star bistros, and I guess the Spindletop Café counts.

"That was very nice of her," Mom says, like, "I know I didn't pay for that."

I feel guilty, because I'm not telling Mom the real reason why Mrs. Walker took the Cheetah Girls to the Spindletop. It was because she felt sorry for the whole *tragedia* that happened between us and the Cash Money Girls.

Sighing, I realize that the real reason I don't want to tell Mom what happened is because she'll just be, like, "I told you so." She doesn't really want me to be in the Cheetah Girls, because she says it's only gonna bring me heartache.

I don't want to admit it, but in a way she's right. We sure have had a lot of heartaches, bellyaches, and toothaches, if you ask me. But it's all worth it when things go right. And anyway, it's *my* life, not hers. Truth is, I'm afraid she's gonna take the same attitude about me and ballet.

"What's the name of the restaurant?" Mom asks me.

"Um, it's called the Spindletop. It has a revolving rooftop, so when you're sitting inside, looking out at all the skyscrapers, it seems like they're moving—but it's because you're rotating!"

"I'm dizzy just listening to you," Mom says, dismissing me.

Cuchifrita, Ballerina

Suddenly, I'm getting annoyed with her. So what if it wasn't the Gay Paree Café or something? Maybe if she would've taken me to Paris with her, I would *know* what a five-star bistro is!

I wince at the thought. I don't want to go anywhere with Mom. I would rather spend fifty years in a Chinese torture dungeon!

"Kashmir took me to the most fabulous restaurant in Paris," Mom says, wistfully, calling the tycoon by his first name. "La Butte Chaillot."

It sounds like she said, "Da butt Shall Move," so I don't try to pronounce the name of the restaurant, but I want to seem interested in her *historia*. I must have ballet on my brain, because it seems like I can't concentrate on anything. "What kind of food did they have at, um, the restaurant?" I ask, knowing how Mom loves to talk about food, even though she doesn't eat much.

"Oh," Mom says, perking up, like she's surprised I'm interested. "The chef is *renowned*— Guy Petit Le Fleur. The food is what you call country bistro cuisine—sophisticated, of course. . . ."

Of course, I think to myself, wondering if

Mom is gonna have any skin left once she takes that contraption off her face.

"The snails were so delicious—oh, and the oysters with cream *mousse*. I could have stayed in Paris and never come home," Mom says, like she really means it.

Now I'm angry. She likes that tycoon of hers better than she does me! And did she say she ate *moose*? Well, I wish it ate her and she didn't come back!

Suddenly, I feel guilty for thinking something so awful. After all, Mom let me go to Houston and spend Thanksgiving with my friends. I should be grateful!

Suddenly, just as I'm about to broach the subject of ballet, I feel a wave of light-headedness come over me. Maybe it's because I haven't eaten since last night's dinner. The twins' family kept feeding us so much that I must have gained at least five pounds! So I made up my mind then and there to stop eating until I lost the weight again.

Not eating on the airplane was easy—their food is totally wack—but I guess Miss Cuchifrita's gotta eat her three square meals every day, 'cuz now I'm feeling dizzy. I clutch at the newspaper as it falls from my hand and drops to the floor.

"What's that?" Mom asks, not noticing my little fit of dizziness. Recovering before she sees me stumble, I grab the newspaper off the floor and show it to her.

"Um, look at this," I say, fumbling to find the page with the ad for American Ballet Theatre. I try to remember to breathe while Mom looks at the ad, so I don't pass out altogether.

"So, what do you want to show me?"

"Um," I say, feeling my throat constricting, "I want to try out for the Junior Ballet Corps Division."

"Chanel, you haven't taken ballet classes with Mrs. Bermudez in two years. What makes you think you can get into the Junior Corps?"

"I practice all the time—really hard," I say, flustered.

"You call doing a few *tendu* exercises every once in a while practicing?" Mom retorts in a nasty voice.

I try not to let Mom's remark get to me, but my voice cracks. "I do practice! I do my warm-up exercises five times a week, then *adagios* at the barre in the exercise studio, then floor exercises, and then—"

Mom cuts me off before I finish—which is good, 'cuz I was about to blurt out that I can't work at the barre in the exercise studio because *she* is always in there, practicing her stupid belly dancing just to impress her boyfriend!

"If you want to try out, fine—but don't expect me to pay for any more classes," she says, without putting up any more of a fight.

I can't believe it! She didn't even try to talk me out of it! I feel guilty and sad now, for thinking all those bad things about Mom. All she ever really wants is for me to do what she says. I'll bet if I went along with her more often, we wouldn't be fighting all the time.

"But I don't think you should try out for the Junior Corps—" she blurts out, deciding after all to argue with me. I should have known it was too good to be true!

"But that's the only way I'm gonna get in without paying!" I whine.

"The Junior Ballet Corps Division?" Mom repeats, surprised. "You want to get into the *professional* company?" She gives me a look like she thinks I'm cuckoo, then says, "And what about your singing group?"

I stand there, with tears forming in my eyes. "I—I'll just have to do both," I stammer. "I'm fourteen years old. This is my last chance to see if I can be a ballerina, *Mami*. I want to try."

Mom softens. "I don't think you're ready for it, Chanel, but I'm not going to stop you. If you get in, then we'll talk about it." Then she adds, "Maybe your father will pay for everything."

She looks away and pretends to read her magazine, but I think she's embarrassed that she snapped again about Daddy. She always tries to pretend it doesn't bother her that he loves Princess Pamela and not her.

Right now, I don't want to think about Mom and Daddy fighting, or how sad I feel because I don't see Daddy as much as I'd like. Obviously, he doesn't love *me* anymore, either.

"Thank you, *Mami*, you'll see—I'm gonna get into the Junior Ballet Corps Division—then I'll decide if I want to be a ballerina or not." I bend over to touch her ponytail.

"What are you thanking me for?" Mom asks.

"Um . . ." I stutter, because I am still scheming, "because . . . you're going to give me money to buy new pointe shoes?"

"Ohhh . . ." Mom says, pausing. "Oh, all right. Go get my purse."

"Yes! I love you, *Mamí*!" I prance all the way to her bedroom to get her purse, and when I open the door, I gasp. I can't believe all the shopping bags flung around the room! She must have brought back everything but the Eiffel Tower!

I feel my temples getting hot again. How could she buy Pucci a scooter? *I wonder if she brought me back anything?*

I resist the urge to peek in the shopping bags. That's all I need is for her to catch me — I'd be grounded for life. Maybe she's gonna surprise me later, I think, trying to calm down. What counts now is that I'm gonna show her—and everybody else—that I can be a ballerina.

I hear the doorbell ring again, and Mom yells, "What is this, Halloween?"

I run to the door and answer it. "It's the delivery guy with flowers, *Mamí*," I say, feeling my face get flushed, because I know the flowers are not for me. I mean, Krusher doesn't know where I live, *está bien?* And who else would ever send me flowers?

Cuchifrita, Ballerina

"Thank you," I say to the guy, and take the big box tied with bright red ribbon to Mom. I love boxes with big ribbons!

"Ooo!" Mom says, her face lighting up, because we both know who the flowers are from—Mr. Tycoon. Mr. Sheik. Mr. Moneybags.

I don't know if I'm gonna make it as a Cheetah Girl, or as a ballerina, or even something else I don't know about yet. But one day, I'm going to get more flowers than anybody has ever seen—even if I have to send them to myself!

Chapter 3

After I clean up my room, dust off the twenty-seven dolls in my collection, and put them back on the shelves, I kneel down and say a silent prayer: *Please let me get into the American Ballet Theatre Junior Corps.*

Then I tiptoe over to my red Princess phone to call Daddy. I want to see him and Princess Pamela, and hear all about Transylvania, and about Dracula's relatives. If Daddy is back, then he is probably at one of his restaurants— The Return of the Killer Tacos—because Daddy works even on Sundays.

"Chanel!" yells Mom from her bedroom. I feel so guilty about calling Daddy that I automatically hang up the receiver, even though someone has already picked up the phone. Mom would be upset if she knew I was calling Daddy—and even more upset if I talked to Princess Pamela.

"Coming, *Mamí*!" I yell back, so she doesn't get suspicious. Suddenly, I get excited—maybe Mom's calling for me because she brought me a present from Paris! The last time she went there, she brought me these coolio French berets—which I love, even though when it's really hot they make me break out around my forehead.

Right now I can't afford to break out, because I want to look perfect for my audition at the American Ballet Theatre—if I even get one, of course. The judges at dance auditions sit very prim and proper, while you dance and sweat your heart out—and they're judging every *adagio* step, every *petit allegro*, every *port de bras* arm movement—which should be as graceful as a swan floating on a pond.

I prance down the hallway to Mom's bedroom, fantasizing that I'm Princess Aurora in *Sleeping Beauty*, waiting to get kissed so I can wake up after sleeping for a thousand years. *"Sí, Mamí?"* I say cheerfully, peeking into her bedroom. Now that she has given me fifty dollars to buy a new pair of pointe shoes, I don't feel so mad at her for bringing Pucci that stupid scooter.

"I got you something," Mom says, handing me a shiny pink box. It can't be another French beret, because the box is too big.

I feel my heart fluttering as I open the flesh-colored satin ribbon—which reminds me of the beautiful ribbons I sew so carefully onto my pointe shoes. "Ooo," I sigh as I tear into the creamy layers of tissue paper and see the pink netting underneath. "Aaaaah, *Mamí*!" I exclaim as I hold up a powder pink tutu. *La más bonita!*

"Nobody makes a tutu like the French. *Nadie*. It has sixteen rows of tulle net." Mom is trying to act nonchalant. Then she abruptly barks, "I've gotta get this thing off my face. I'll be right back!"

I think Mom ran into the bathroom because she doesn't want me to hug her.

I try not to let the disappointment show in my face when she comes back out of her private bathroom. Now she sits in front of her vanity table, and opens one of the fifty jars she has lined up in neat rows.

Cuchifrita, Ballerina

That's when I get a good look at her. *Cuatro* yuks! Her face looks lighter than the rest of her body! I think that hockey mask sucked all the oxygen out of her, like a vampire or something. She's lucky she still has skin on her face after wearing that suction trap!

"You know, Chanel, I always wanted you to be a ballerina," Mom says, heaving a deep sigh and slathering cream all over her face. I think it would be better for you than being in that singing group." Then she frowns. "Just because Bubbles doesn't have the discipline for ballet, doesn't mean *you* shouldn't do it."

"I know, *Mamí*," I say, getting teary-eyed, because I think she is finally trying to tell me that I'm good at something. "Thank you for the tutu."

"De nada, amor," Mom says, beaming at my reflection in her mirror. "You know, the French invented ballet, too."

"Really?" I say, surprised.

"Of course, Chanel—why do you think all the movements are in French—*plié, pirouette*?" Mom sounds a little annoyed with me. *"Por qué?"*

I stand dumbfounded, clutching my new tutu, because I can't think of an answer. I should have known the reason why Mom liked ballet. She likes *anything* French—even five-day-old *croissants*!

"I knew that, *Mamí*, I just forgot," I say, telling a *poco* fib-eroni. I know God will forgive me. I try to seem interested in Mom's trip to Paris, so she will get off my case.

"Did you go to anyplace interesting, like the Eiffel Tower?" I ask.

"No, Chanel," Mom snipes. "I did not go to the Eiffel Tower—that's for tourists."

Now I feel like a complete *babosa*, because of course only tourists would go see the Eiffel Tower, and Mom does *not* consider herself a tourist in Paris. The silence is very uncomfortable. Then, *gracias gooseness*, Mom says, "We did go to the Musée d'Orsay—you know, most of the exhibits there come from the Louvre."

"*Sí, Mamí*," I say, nodding. I wonder what the Louvre is, but I don't ask. Knowing Mom and Mr. Tycoon, it must be someplace where snobby people go.

"Oh, the sculpture!" she sighs wistfully. I never heard her speak that way about art, but I guess now that Mr. Tycoon is her boyfriend, she's learning a lot of new things. "When you walk in the center aisle, there is this wonderful series of busts—thirty-six of them."

Did Mom say busts? Does she mean they had ladies' breasts in the museum? I don't say anything, because I don't know what she's talking about, and I don't want her to think I'm stupid or something.

"Then I saw this bronze statue that took my breath away—'Young Dancer of Fourteen,' by Edgar Degas. The statue looked just like you, Chanel, with her feet poised in second position, and long braids down her back. That's why I went and bought you the tutu."

I feel the tears welling up in my eyes, so I look down at my shoes, but the change in Mom's voice snaps me out of my sadness.

"I still don't think you should try out for the Junior Ballet Corps Division yet," she pronounces in a tone of warning. "But if you've got your mind made up, you'd better start practicing every day."

"I will," I say defensively. "Can I use the exercise studio now?"

"Okay, but I wanna get in there soon and do my belly dancing," Mom says, rubbing her calf. "I didn't exercise the whole time I was in Paris, and I ate like a *puerco*. I know I'm gonna pay for it on the scale."

"You don't look like *un puerco*," I say jokingly. Mom is very skinny, but she is always imagining that she puts on weight.

Suddenly I think, again, *maybe I put on weight, too!* I tried not to eat too much food in Houston, but you know southern hospitality—and besides, it was Thanksgiving. . . . I hold the tutu up against my stomach and look at myself from the side in the mirror. My butt is sticking out even more than usual!

"Tuck your butt in," Mom warns me, like she's reading my mind.

Now I remember why else I gave up ballet—it wasn't *just* because of Bubbles. I thought my butt stuck out too much for me to be a ballerina! I hold the tutu tighter against my chest, and try not to think about it.

"I'm going to exercise now," I tell Mom. Trying to fight back tears, I blurt out, "I've never forgotten that you took me to see *Sleeping Beauty* when I was little."

"Did I?" Mom says, like she doesn't remember.

"I'm already fourteen, *Mami*, and I want to

be Sleeping Beauty—Princess Aurora, I mean—before it's too late."

"That's true—you are getting older, and the decisions you make now will affect the rest of your life—that's all I've been trying to tell you, *mija*."

"I know, *Mamí*," I sigh, then run out of her bedroom, because I want to cry. Suddenly I don't trust her. Why didn't she give me a hard time about auditioning for American Ballet Theatre? Maybe she wants me to get back into ballet because she thinks I'm a terrible singer. *Maybe that's why she doesn't want me to be in the Cheetah Girls.*

Mom is waiting for me to finish exercising, but right this minute I'm too upset to concentrate. I run into my bedroom instead, and pick up the receiver on my red Princess telephone. While the phone rings, I hold my breath, because I know that Bubbles probably doesn't want to talk to me. She hardly said a word to me the whole way home from the airport.

"Hi, *mamacita*," I squeal into the receiver, trying to sound cheerful. "I, um, was wondering if you would bring Toto and come with me to the Blessing of the Insects and Their Four-Legged

Friends Ceremony," I say. When Bubbles doesn't say anything, I add, "I'm gonna bring Mr. Cuckoo—'cuz stupid Pucci won't do it."

"Sure," Bubbles says, surprisingly cheerful. "That'll give Toto something to do. He's been walking around the house sulking because I left him alone all week. And by the way . . ."

I know that tone of voice. It means Bubbles has good news. No wonder she didn't yell at me about Houston! "Mom's got this tight idea," she says proudly. "I'll tell you when I see you."

"Okay!" I can't wait to hear about *Madrina*'s great idea. She always has *la dopa* ideas—that's why she's our manager, and my godmother for life.

"I'll meet you in front of the cathedral at five o'clock," Bubbles says. Then she yells to Toto, who is barking in the background, "Hold your hot dogs, Toto, I'm coming!"

When I become a famous ballerina, and get my own apartment, the first thing I'm going to do is get a dog just like Toto! For a second, I get mad again at Mom, then realize that I shouldn't be. It's not her fault she's allergic to dog and cat fur. And besides, she did buy me a tutu in Paris! How many girls at American

Cuchifrita, Ballerina

Ballet Theatre can say that, huh? *Nadie, está bien?* Nobody but me.

Oops—I guess I'm not in American Ballet Theatre *yet*. But you just wait until I leap across the stage—I'll be the most beautiful Dominican Princess Aurora the world has ever seen! I pick up my new tutu and stare at it. It's the most beautiful one I've ever seen. I guess Mom really does love me, even though sometimes I think she is disappointed in me.

Staring at my tutu, I remember again the time Mom took me to see *Sleeping Beauty* at Lincoln Center. I was five years old, and wearing a pretty pink dress with ribbons in my hair. Mom kept showing me off to all the ladies in the balcony where we were sitting. It was one of the few times I remember going anywhere alone with Mom—Pucci was too little to go, and Daddy was working at his restaurant. He was always working back then.

I loved *Sleeping Beauty*, even though I got very scared when the wicked fairy Carabosse appeared—uninvited—and put the curse on the baby princess, telling her parents that she would die on her sixteenth birthday.

What will happen to *me* on my sixteenth

birthday? I don't want to think about that right now. Instead, I carefully put down my new tutu, and slip into my black footless cotton unitard and my old pink ballet shoes. Uh-oh—they're a little tight. I reach under my bed, feeling for the shoe box that contains the can of shoe spray I use to stretch my shoes. I can't afford to get any blisters right before my audition!

Dragging the box from under the bed, I take out my very first pair of pointe shoes—all moth-eaten and old, and so tiny! Mom bought them for me when I was seven years old. . . .

I start crying like a baby, and plop to the floor. Mom was so disappointed when I stopped going to Ballet Hispanico. I remember that Bubbles didn't like our teacher, Mrs. Bermudez. She thought she was too mean. I can still remember Bubbles poking her mouth out at Mrs. Bermudez. In ballet school, the teacher conducts the class and students are expected to follow whatever she says. Bubbles hated that. She doesn't like teachers telling her what to do.

I can see Mrs. Bermudez now—her black hair slicked back into a tight bun on top of her head, and her skinny lips accented by red lipstick. "Don't let your backside stick out, Chanel!" she would say sternly when I did my *grands pliés*, which are very deep, and require the upper body to remain perfectly straight.

Wiping away my tears, I put my old pointe shoes back, and take out the can of shoe stretch spray I was looking for all along.

After spraying inside my ballet shoes, I walk on *demi-pointe* to the exercise studio until my shoes dry and mold to my feet. I look at my profile in the exercise studio mirror. Suddenly it hits me—not only my butt, but my stomach is sticking out! I suck it in and stand up straight. I'm not going to eat dinner tonight—even if Mom makes my favorite Dominican-style *arroz con pollo*! No dinner for Miss Cuchifrita!

Now it's time to stop fussing around, or I'll be late meeting Bubbles at the cathedral, and I don't want her yelling at me. I'm always late for everything, it seems. I put my hand on the barre and start my *pliés*, then do my *tendu* exercises to warm up my feet, then *dégagés* and *ronds des jambes*, on the floor and off—making sure to keep my heel forward. That is so hard, I hate it!

My favorite part of the workout is the cooldown. That's when I do my *grand battements* in each direction—these are big, controlled kicks, and they're fun to do. I can hear Mrs. Bermudez in my head: "Chanel, don't lean forward—stay straight." When you're doing *grand battements*, you're only supposed to move the hip sockets and below—the upper body should be perfectly still. "Think of the beautiful swan swimming across the pond," Mrs. Bermudez used to tell us.

I am a beautiful swan, I tell myself. Then, suddenly, a voice inside me shrieks, *What if I'm really the ugly duckling?*

I put my arms high over head, making my movements as graceful as ever, moving my arms from fifth position to first and open to second position, then gloat in the mirror at my reflection. I am *not* an ugly ducking—because no ugly duckling in the world does *ports de bras* as graceful as mine!

I sure hope I got the audition appointment—because if I get to try out, there's no doubt this *girlita* is gonna make it into the Junior Corps!

Chapter 4

The Blessing of the Insects and Their Four-Legged Friends Ceremony at the Cathedral of St. John the Divine, at 112th Street and Amsterdam Avenue, is very popular—*muy populáro*. It coincides with the Feast of St. Cucaracha of Washington Heights, a saint who loved animals and nature. Of course, St. Cucaracha is one of *my* favorite saints, too. I know Mom would croak if she heard me say that, but it's true! She hates animals because they shed a lot of hair, which makes her sneeze and gets all over the furniture. I'm sorry, but I think Mom sheds more hair than any animal I've ever met.

Standing at the bottom of the steps in front of the beautiful cathedral, I lift my heels so that I can balance myself on my tippy-toes and look over the crowd. Sure enough, I see Bubbles coming toward me, wearing a red knit hat with a big red pom-pom on top. It bops to her beat, like a cherry on an ice cream sundae. I guess there's no way I would be able to miss her in that outfit!

"Where's Mr. Cuckoo?" Bubbles asks, before she even gives one of her usual flippy salutations.

"I didn't want to bring his cage," I explain in a whiny voice. I don't mean to sound like that, but I'm still nervous about Bubbles being mad at me, even though I'm trying to pretend I'm not. *Qué broma*, what a joke. I mean, the tension between us is thicker than nutty Nutella spread, *está bien*? I open my backpack, so Bubbles can see Mr. Cuckoo nestled in a towel inside.

"Ohhh, he looks smaller," Bubbles says, concerned, like he's not being taken care of properly or something.

"He's *bigger* than he was when we bought him," I insist.

"Oh. Well, maybe it's the way he looks wrapped up in that towel—you know, the background contrast is so close to his color,"

Cuchifrita, Ballerina

Bubbles says, like she's doing an assignment in one of our art composition classes at school.

Toto stands up and rests his paws on my leg. "Hi, Toto!" I exclaim, bending down to fix his cheetah jacket, which is riding up toward his neck. "Oh, you need a haircut, boo-boo!"

"Why don't *you* give it to him?" Bubbles asks, *muy sarcástico.*

"If you want me to, I can do it later," I reply.

"Mom is gonna take him to the Doggies Can Be Down Spa next week, so he'll get a cut there and a pawd-icure," Bubbles explains. I wish I went to as many different beauty parlors as Toto goes to, *está bien?*

"Are you going up?" asks this lady behind me, like she's annoyed because Bubbles and I are just hanging out on the cathedral steps.

I turn around to look at her, and catch the Wicked Witch expression on her face. *La gente* in *Nueva York* can be so rude! But I can't be mad at her for long, because the parrot atop her shoulder squawks at me, "Hello, pretty!"

"He's so beautiful!" I exclaim, admiring the parrot's red plumage, which is brighter than my favorite shade of S.N.A.P.S. lipstick—Raven Red. "What kind of parrot is he?"

"It's a girl," the Wicked Witch lady snaps back.

"Oh, I'm sorry."

"That's okay," the lady says, softening. "She's an Eclectus Parrot—the males and females have completely different colors. The males are bright green."

"Oh," I say, fascinated. "Has he—I mean, *she*—ever been to St. John's for a blessing before?"

"No, it's her first time—and from the looks of this crowd, it may be her last," the Wicked Witch lady snipes at me, looking around in disgust.

It is getting pretty crowded. I mean, St. John's Cathedral looks like it's going to the dogs . . . and cats and fish and—"Ooo, look, Bubbles, somebody brought an elephant!"

"That's nutso," Bubbles squawks. Toto starts barking, because the crowd is getting too close to him, so Bubbles picks him up, even though he weighs a ton. "Come here, Fatso," she says, rubbing his underbelly as he lies floppy-style in her arms.

The dumbo jumbo elephant is flanked by police officers on horses, and luckily, is ushered through a side entrance of the cathedral—or else we would have had a stampede!

"I wonder whose pet that is?" I ask in disbelief. I mean, there are so many rich people in New York, maybe some little boy who lives in a castle is the proud owner of Mr. Dumbo Jumbo. As much as I love pets, the one thing I wouldn't want is an elephant—because they stink too much, and I don't like smelly things around me all the time.

"I heard they're expecting four thousand people," the Wicked Witch says, turning slowly back to the front so that her prized parrot doesn't get jolted from her shoulder. "But it looks more like forty thousand if you ask me."

It's a good thing nobody is asking her. I look around at the crowd again—and see kids with fishbowls filled with lizards, frogs, and fish.

"There's a Chihuahua, Chuchie," Bubbles say, turning to her right.

"*Ay, Dios*—there are three of them!" I say, counting the three ladies with kerchiefs holding my favorite little dogs in their arms. As much as I love Toto, what I really want is a Chihuahua, imported straight from Mexico and into my arms!

"We're finally moving," moans the lady, giving me and Bubbles our cue to move up the cathedral steps.

Even though I'm eager to hear about *Madrina*'s great idea, I'm more anxious to tell Bubbles about my decision to try out for the American Ballet Theatre. I just want to get it over with, *está bien?*

"*Mamí* brought me a tutu from Paris," I say, turning to Bubbles with a smile. I can feel the squigglies starting in my stomach again.

"Really?" Bubbles asks, bouncing Toto up and down in her arms.

"In that big city of soufflé and dreams, why would she get you a tutu?" Bubbles asks, crinkling her nose.

"Y-you know, *Mamí* wants me to be a . . . ballerina," I stammer.

"Yeah, well, wants and wishes are best bestowed by fairy godmothers with magic wands," Bubbles snorts.

"*I* want to be a ballerina, too," I blurt out. Immediately, I feel my stomach get more squiggly.

"Chuchie—your days of sashay on the pirouette tip are long over. Don't you think, pink?" Bubbles asks, raising her eyebrow at me.

"No, I don't," I reply, holding my ground. "I'm going to try and get into the American Ballet Theatre." Wincing, I quickly add, "the

Cuchifrita, Ballerina

Junior Ballet Corps Division." I don't want Bubbles to think I've completely gone cuckoo.

"Are you serious?" Bubbles asks, surprised.

"Sí, mamacita."

"Well, I hope this crusade is a lot better planned than your songwriting fiasco," Bubbles says, poking her mouth out.

There. She finally said it. It is all *my* fault that *we* wrote a song *together* called "It's Raining Benjamins," and copied some of the words from the Cash Money Girls. If Bubbles was supposed to know so much about songwriting, then how come *she* didn't know about copyright infringement?

"Bubbles, I-I didn't write the song by myself," I say, stuttering. "You said yourself that I only wrote two lines of it."

Bubbles shoots me a look, and I realize that I've made a big boo-boo. See, Dorinda told me what Bubbles said behind my back, and I guess I shouldn't have repeated it to Bubbles's face.

"Dorinda didn't tell me—I, um, just knew you felt that way," I say, feeling my face turn deep red.

"If Dorinda didn't tell you, then how did you know I said that?" Bubbles asks. "I guess you are just the queen of the crystal ball?"

"Um . . . I guess because . . . she didn't tell me anything! *Nada*," I say, trying to tell a *poco* fib-eroni about my fib-eroni. If I don't stop, I'm gonna start confusing myself!

"But see, that's not the point, Chuchie," Bubbles says, getting so angry at me that she doesn't care if everyone around us on the cathedral stairs hears. "The point to this joint, is that you wanted to write this song *together*, when *I* could have been thinking up an *original* song."

"Yeah, but you came up with some of the words, too!" I hiss at Bubbles.

"Yeah, but I'm not the one who had a so-called dream about Benjamins falling from the sky, and you and I grabbing them like a couple of Mary Poppins wanna-bes!" Bubbles is glaring at me now, and pointing. "The idea for the song came from *you*."

"I *did* have the dream, Bubbles!" I say, teary-eyed. "*Te juro.* I swear. You and I were standing under an umbrella together—"

"You shoulda known that dream was a fake, because I never stand under an umbrella with you—you always make the umbrella bop up and down and get my hair wet!"

Cuchifrita, Ballerina

Now I'm really crying. "I'm not going to write any more songs with you!"

"Is that a promise?" Bubbles asks, not backing down. She hates it when I start crying, because it makes her feel like a bully—which she is. Bubbles the bully!

Now the peeps on the steps are staring at us. I turn and see this lady holding a big black cat. The cat starts meowing right in my face. *Ay, Dios mío*, his teeth look like fangs! That is a bad omen. I can tell something bad is going to happen. I gulp really hard and turn quickly from the black cat. Why does the lady with her stupid cat have to stand in back of *me*? This is not what I need right now!

All of sudden Bubbles blurts out, "How are you gonna have time for it?"

"Time for what?" I ask, still scared by the black cat and his meowing.

He won't shut up. *Cáyate!*

"Time to go to school, work in my mom's store to pay off what you still owe your mom, rehearse with the Cheetah Girls, *and* practice ballet?"

"Well, it's not like we're doing anything with the Cheetah Girls right now," I say wincing.

Bubbles shoots me a look, like, "Who says?"

"What happened?"

"That's what I wanted to tell you," Bubbles shoots back, sounding like Miss Clucky, the gossip lady on television. "My mom is going to call Def Duck Records, and ask them if we can put on an informal showcase for the New York staff—you know, give them a taste of our flava, so they can get with the program—and maybe the producer they've assigned us to—Mouse Almighty—will get excited, alrighty."

"That's a good idea," I say, my eyes opening wide.

"So, you'd better stick around for the cause, whenever it goes down," Bubbles says, licking her lips.

"*Claro que sí*, Bubbles! Of course, I will. But I'm still going to try to get into American Ballet Theatre—this is my last chance, last dance."

Bubbles just eyes me, then blurts out, "I don't know how you can do it. Remember our ballet teacher, Mrs. Bermudez?"

"Yeah," I say, chuckling. "She used to tell you, '*Plié* like a swan, Galleria, not like an ugly duckling!'"

Bubbles winces at this memory, which makes me feel like *una babosa* for even bringing it up. I'm so stupid sometimes!

At last we are inside the cathedral. Carefully, I take Mr. Cuckoo out of my backpack so he can breathe. I cup my palms together, so he has a little place to hang out.

We're just in time, because the service is about to begin. "Ladies and gentlemen, girls and boys, may I introduce the Paul Winter Consort jazz group," says a lady into the microphone. Everyone starts clapping. "They will be doing a special perfomance piece—'Earth Mass'—for this joyous occasion. And please welcome our featured dancers, from the Omega and Forces of Nature troupes. Today, Reverend Harry Pritchett will officiate over our blessing ceremony, to promote harmony and peace between man, animal, and *bug*!"

My eyes are glued to the dancers, who prance in the front of the high altar and do a beautiful routine. The ceilings in the cathedral are so high that the sound of meows and barks echoes over the music, making the whole place sound like a haunted castle. I whisper to Bubbles that I want to move closer. I don't want to miss one movement, one *grande battement*, from this troupe of dancers.

Suddenly, we hear the sound of the trumpet. *Oh, no*—the elephant is now being brought to the front of the high altar from the side entrance. He takes up all the room in front of us. I let out a sigh of disappointment. Bubbles shrugs her shoulders, like, "You know the way things flow in the Big Apple."

Sometimes I just hate everyone—and now, I'm even angry at all the animals. I just want to see the dancers! Mr. Cuckoo starts squiggling around in my palms. I look at him and stroke his head, then remember why I'm here—so he can have a blessed life, and be protected from the evil forces in the world. "St. Cucaracha will look over you, *precioso*," I coo to him. I wish he was *my* pet, not Pucci's.

Now the lady leading the service is instructing us to stand in line, so that Reverend Pritchett can bless each and every animal. At this rate, we will be here till midnight—especially since Bubbles and I are so far back in the line.

With all this time to spare, I figure it won't hurt to say a prayer for myself. I put Mr. Cuckoo back in my backpack for a second, then cross myself and close my eyes. *Por favor, Dios,* I think, *please let me get into the American Ballet Theatre. And please protect the Cheetah Girls, and let us become famous, so we can travel all over the world, and sing to all of the creatures that you created. Amen.*

When I open my eyes, I see that Bubbles is staring at me. "I hope you said a prayer for me, too, Miss Cuchifrita Ballerina!"

"I did," I tell Bubbles, and smile at her.

Bubbles giggles. I feel like I can take a deep breath, because someone let the air out of the hot-air balloon. "I like that," I whisper to her.

"Like what?" Bubbles whispers.

"Miss Cuchifrita Ballerina," I say, beaming. I know Bubbles doesn't think I can get into the ballet company, and I know she doesn't understand why I have to do this, but I do know that she is the only sister I have—even if we aren't real sisters. Like Bubbles says, we are the dynamic duo, bound till death!

"I just hope you don't leap into the great beyond and land on your head, like you did in the twins' bedroom down in Houston," Bubbles says, bringing up that painful memory again.

"The area rug slipped," I protest.

"Don't get flippy with me, Miss Slippy," Bubbles retorts.

"I like my other nickname better." I wince.

Bubbles smirks, and says, "Okay, Miss Cuchifrita Ballerina—pirouette till payday!"

I can't believe Bubbles read my mind—but why am I surprised? Like I said, we are the dynamic duo, flapping in the wind with or without our capes!

Chapter 5

It is so cold, icicles are hanging off trees. Pursued by a magic troop of leaden soldiers, a handsome prince appears out of the darkness. Recognizing my true love, the Lilac Fairy shows Krusher—who is wearing a black cape and eye patch—a hologramma vision of me sleeping in the enchanted forest. Krusher begs the Lilac Fairy to show him where the real me lies. He smiles, and serenades the Lilac Fairy with an a capella version of his song, "She's My Girl."

The Lilac Fairy is captivated, and agrees to guide Krusher through the wicked fairy Carabosse's magic world—past the rats and the captive fairy children that were stolen from their homeland, to the place where I'm lying, in the new pink tutu Mom just bought me, asleep in a bed of pink flowers. Krusher does his famous double-neck move and supa-dupa split—snowflakes melting off his leather pants in the process—then kisses me gently on the lips. . . .

Which wakes me up. At first, I have sleep in my eyes, and rub them hard, but I recognize Krusher from his new album cover, and gaspitate because I cannot believe my eyes. I think the wicked fairy Carabosse is playing another trick on me. After all, it was she, disguised as a handsome suitor, who put the spell on me in the first place! Krusher smiles, and I recognize his big, beautiful teeth, and know that it is not Carabosse pretending to be him.

I smile back, my heart melting. Krusher whips me into his arms and we dance through the forest. I didn't know Krusher could dance ballet, but he leaps and pirouettes like the true prince he is. Suddenly, Krusher pulls me up on his shoulders, like I weigh no more than a feather. I hold my head up to the clouds, and extend my legs in a perfect split as he swirls and twirls.

Spinning round and round, I suddenly fall from his arms onto the ground, because Carabosse's evil spell has not been broken! The animals run from the forest, because there is a loud buzzing noise filling the air, a noise that is louder than my scream. . . .

Suddenly, I realize that the buzzing noise is

the sound of my stupid alarm clock going off,
and that my beautiful dream has turned into a
Nightmare in the Enchanted Forest. I fight off
the breathless feeling in my chest. *Ay, Dios,*
another omen—the *brujas* are trying to tell me
something. . . .

I sit on the edge of my bed, frozen, then suddenly it dawns on me. *La bruja*—the good
witch—is trying to guide me out of the forest
and away from danger. She's trying to tell me
that I am not Princess Aurora yet, that I'd better
go practice so I can become her one day for real!

I turn and look at my alarm clock—the neon-
lit numbers are shining bright and steady. It is
six o'clock in the morning. I have an hour and
a half to practice and get ready for school. I
don't want to practice. *Yo quiero dormir más!*
Sleeping Beauty is calling me.

Coming out of my dream haze, I get frozen
with fear. I know in my heart that soon it will
be too late for me to pursue my dream. I jump
off my bed and quietly slip on my unitard, then
tiptoe to the studio and turn on the lights. Yes,
I'm yawning the whole time, but doing my ballet warm-up will wake me up out of my trance.

I have to write a letter to Krusher, I think,

smiling to my reflection in the mirror as I begin my pliés at the barre, bending my knees as deep as I can while keeping my posture perfect.

What if Krusher doesn't write me back? I do my stretches, alternating legs and bending over, taking deep sighs.

If I don't get into the Junior Corps, then I don't want to live. I won't even care about meeting Krusher. By the time I get to my *frappés*—bending the knee and flexing my foot so it's at a perfect right angle to my leg, I have forgotten about my fears. This is what I love about ballet. It takes me to *un otro mundo*, another world, in which I am the star—like Giselle, Raymonda, or Princess Aurora—a star whom everybody wants to kiss and love forever.

Now I feel excited, because I'm going to buy new pointe shoes after school today. I also have to go to the American Ballet Theatre, and find out if I get to audition for the Junior Corps Division. Suddenly, I get a squiggle in my stomach again. What am I going to wear? I know I'm only going to see the registrar, but every impression counts.

Red—*rojo*—my favorite color. That's what I'll wear, from head to toe. It always makes me feel my "growl power," and people always stop to look at me, because red makes everybody feel happy.

Looking down at my nails, I see that they are chipped. I'd better put on a coat of S.N.A.P.S. "Maui Wowie" Nail Polish for good measure. It's a pretty shade of Frosted Lime Green. I love it because it's not too dark, so it doesn't draw too much attention to my short, stubby nails.

After I shower and dress, I go to the kitchen to get my breakfast. I hear Mom yelling at Pucci, "No—you eat a bowl of cereal with one English muffin or one Pop Tart, but you are not going to eat both, *entiendes?*"

Just swell-io. Mom is in a bad mood. But when I walk into the dining room where she and Pucci are sitting eating breakfast, I can see why—her face looks like the girl's in *The Exorcist*. It's covered with little red bumps!

"What are you looking at?" Mom says, teary-eyed.

"What happened? *Qué pasó?*" I ask, staring at the pimply *pobrecita* who used to be my beautiful mom.

"Don't worry, I'm going to sue those charlatans who manufacture that *Vivre de Glamour* vibrating contraption!" Mom says, her voice squeaking.

I feel so bad for Mom that I don't even ask for my lunch money. I'm not going to eat lunch today anyway. Gotta lose some more weight before my big audition—*if* I get it.

"What's that on your nails, Chanel? You look like you have ten green thumbs!" Mom snaps at me.

"Um, it's a shade called 'Maui Wowie,' *Mamí*," I stammer.

"*Mamí*, can I ride my scooter to school?" Pucci asks, interrupting us.

"No! You walk to school just like everybody else!" Mom yells.

"Moham's mother lets him take *his* to school," Pucci blurts out.

"Moham's mother is a—" Mom says, then stops herself.

Knowing Mom, she was gonna say something nasty, and big-mouthed Pucci would go to school and blurt it out to Moham, who would get hurt feelings. Ever since Daddy moved out, Pucci doesn't care about anybody else's feelings but his own, and his *boca grande*—big mouth—has gotten even bigger.

He sits there sulking, then says to me, "Mr. Cuckoo doesn't seem any different."

Cuchifrita, Ballerina

"Why should he?" I respond without thinking.

"You took him to get a stupid blessing, that's why," Pucci moans.

Mom grabs Pucci's arm hard, and the cereal box he's holding drops, scattering Cheerios everywhere. "Don't you ever blaspheme the church!"

I wonder what blaspheme means. I'll ask the twins, because they are very religious, but I think it has something to do with saying bad things about the church or something.

Thinking of the twins puts me in mind of the Cheetah Girls. Now that we've spent Thanksgiving together in Houston, it just seems like all five of us should be together all the time. Suddenly, a lightbulb goes off in my head. American Ballet Theatre is in Lincoln Center, right near the twins' school, the Performing Arts Annex at LaGuardia. Maybe next year, the three of us—me, Dorinda and Bubbles—could transfer to the Performing Arts Annex. That way, we'd get to be together all the time—*and* I'd get to be close to the ballet company *and* school.

I feel squiggly in my stomach again. What if I don't get accepted? I pick up the Cheerios and put them back in the box, but Mom screams at Pucci, "Pick up the cereal—and next time, I'll wash your mouth out with soap!"

I say good-bye to Mom (I don't think she hears me anyway), then grab my backpack and run out the door.

When I meet Bubbles and Dorinda before first period, I tell them what happened to Mom.

"I guess Auntie Juanita had to learn the hard way," Bubbles says. "There is a sham in every city, from Paris to Pittsburgh—and that's not pillow talk either!"

"Maybe she didn't use it right?" Dorinda offers.

"Maybe," I say, shrugging my shoulders. It must be hard having a boyfriend, and having to look pretty all the time. Especially a stuffy boyfriend like Mr. Tycoon, who's always dressed like he's going to a Billionaires' Ball or something. Mom is probably afraid she'll turn into a pumpkin after midnight, or lose her slipper—and lose him. Suddenly, I remember the question I wanted to ask Dorinda, about what Mom saw in the Moose d' Horses museum, or whatever it was called.

"Dorinda, what is a bust—I mean, the kind

you see in a museum—it's not like ours, is it?"

Dorinda chuckles. "Chanel—it's sculpture—like, just the upper part," she explains, motioning at her throat. "You know, from there up."

"Why would anybody want to look at heads without bodies—unless it's a spooky museum or something?" I wonder out loud.

"'Cuz it's like, art, that's all. Bronze statues take a lot of work," Dorinda says, then her eyes light up, like she remembers something. Dorinda opens her cheetah backpack, and whips out the cheetah photo album that she bought in Houston. "Look at our scrapbook!" she says proudly.

On the cover, she has glued the letters *The Cheetah Girls*, and inside are all the pictures of us that we've taken together. Under each picture, she has written a caption using a pink pen. "Ooo," I exclaim, as I touch the picture of us in the parking lot after we performed at the Okie-Dokie Corral in Houston. The caption reads, "The Cheetah Girls Get Sassy at the Sassy-sparilla Saloon!"

"Do' Re Mi, I can't believe you did this!" I coo.

"Quiet as it's kept, you really are the brains behind the horse-and-pony show we call the

The Cheetah Girls

Cheetah Girls!" Bubbles quips. "You've just been designated the official keeper of our memories, Do' Re Mi."

"I think we look dope in this one," Do' Re Mi chuckles, pointing to a picture of us performing onstage at the Cheetah-Rama for the Kats and Kittys Klub Halloween Bash. It was the first time we performed together as the Cheetah Girls—and Dorinda split her costume onstage! It was *una catástrofe*, but the audience clapped anyway, because it was all of our friends and Kats and Kittys members from all over the country—well, the East Coast, anyway.

"I guess this picture was, um, taken, before you did the lickety-split onstage, right, *mamacita*?" I giggle.

"Word, I guess so," Dorinda chuckles back.

"How did you get this?" Bubbles asks, surprised.

"Batman," says Dorinda matter-of-factly. See, Derek Ulysses Hambone, who is in our homeroom class, came to the Halloween Bash dressed as Batman. We almost didn't recognize the Caped Crusader without the baggy clothes he usually wears at school. Derek joined the Kats and Kittys Klub because he is goo-goo ga-ga

68

over Bubbles. That's why we nicknamed him the Red Snapper—because he's always snapping at Bubbles' heels, *está bien*? His family has a lot of duckets, so he could afford to join our social club—but he would never have joined if he wasn't trying to get Bubbles to be his Batgirl, *está bien*?

"Good ole Red Snapper came through, huh?" Bubbles says, wistfully staring at our picture. "Which brings me to our latest caper. My mom is gonna call Def Duck Records today, and tell them it's time they laid at least one golden egg—by giving us a little showcase, so the East Coast Big Willies can see what we can do—and maybe Mouse Almighty will get motivated to take a nibble, know what I'm saying? 'Cuz we're tired of playing."

"I heard that," Dorinda retorts.

"So let's meet after school, and I'll give you a full report—because she'll have called me by then on my Miss Wiggy StarWac Phone," Bubbles explains.

Suddenly, I realize I've got a problem—I have to run right after school to get my pointe shoes at On Your Tippytoes, which is right down the block from the American Ballet

Theatre! If I take the number one train, it'll take me half an hour to get there, what with all the crowds bum-rushing the subway stations after school.

"*Está bien.* Okay," I hear myself say out loud—because I don't want to upset Bubbles, now that she has forgiven me for our Houston fiasco. I'll tell her after school.

But wait—how'm I gonna do that? There's no way I can be in two places at once! If I stick around with my crew after school, I'll never make it uptown to get my pointe shoes and get to American Ballet Theatre before they close!

Ay, caramba! What am I going to do now?

Chapter 6

I'm so glad when Italian class is over, because I can talk to Melissa Hernández about my audition. She has been going to ballet school since she was five, and now splits her freshman classes between Fashion Industries East High School and Ballet Hispanico. Her parents worked it out with the principal. Next year, she has to decide if she is going to come here full-time, or go to Ballet Hispanico and commit to becoming a professional ballerina. In many ways, Melissa and I are in the same boat—we're either gonna sink or float!

"*Hola*, Chanel!" she says when she sees me. Melissa is even smaller than I am, and her legs are even more muscular.

"*Hola*," I respond, then blurt out, "I've gotta talk to you."

"*Qué pasa*—what's up?" she asks.

"You know the American Ballet Theatre is having tryouts for its Junior Corps, right?" I say, trying to catch my breath because I'm so excited.

"*Sí*—I heard, but I'm staying at Ballet Hispanico till I decide what to do," Melissa responds, like she thinks I'm telling her because *she* should audition.

"I'm not talking about you, *mija*—I want to try out for it," I say.

"Oh!" Melissa responds like she's really shocked. "*You* wanna try out?"

"*Sí, mija!*" I say. I'm so excited, I want to grab Melissa by the shoulders and jump up and down with her.

"Go for it, if you, um, think you're ready," Melissa says, hesitating.

"You don't think I can do it?" I ask, surprised. If anybody is on my side, I would have thought it would be Melissa.

"No, Chanel, you are a great ballerina—but you haven't been training that much lately, have you? Don't you think maybe you should go back to ballet school for a year or two, *then* try to get into Junior Corps?"

"I wasn't training at all, until a couple of months ago," I admit. "But ever since I started out with the Cheetah Girls, I've been practicing every day, just to make sure my dancing skills were in gear. I'll be okay."

"Then go for it," Melissa says, grabbing me for a hug. "God bless you, *mija*, that you're ready to make that decision. I'm still not ready."

"No?"

"Part of me wants to do it, but another part of me isn't sure I want to devote my whole life to dancing. There are so many other things I want to do."

It's funny, but that's exactly how I feel. I want to be a Cheetah Girl. I want to open a beauty salon—Miss Cuchifrita Curlz. I want to be a ballerina. I want to do it all!

"I'm going by there today to see if I got an audition slot," I say excitedly.

"Good luck," Melissa says, then adds, "If you want to practice together, let me know."

"Would you?" I say, my eyes brightening. "We have a big exercise studio in my apartment, you know—my mother had it built." Suddenly, I wince inside, remembering that

Melissa lives in Washington Heights, just like my *abuela*. Her parents spend every penny they have sending her to ballet school and keeping her in pointe shoes. Why did I have to open my *boca grande* again? Now she's gonna be jealous!

"I would love to. Can I come by at five o'clock today?" Melissa asks hopefully.

"Okay," I say, hugging her tight. "You can come by at five, for sure. *Estás seguro?*"

"*Sí, amor.*"

"Okay, I've gotta go meet Galleria and Dorinda now."

"I'll walk with you," Melissa says, and we head to the front of our school, where my crew is waiting for me.

"It's Melissa—so don't dis her!" Bubbles greets Melissa when she sees us.

"Hi, Galleria!" Melissa shoots back, then turns to me and says, "Tell me what happens—and I'll see you later."

I feel my face turning red as Bubbles asks me, "What's she talking about?"

"Um, I told her that I'm going to try to get into the American Ballet Theatre—the Junior Corps—remember I told you?" I say defensively.

"Oh, yeah—I know," Bubbles says, like,

Cuchifrita, Ballerina

"here goes Chuchie again." She just doesn't take me seriously, no matter what I try to do—write songs, be a ballerina, even that time I tried to make a dress in fifth grade—she just laughed when the seams came out crooked. Sometimes Bubbles acts just like my mother.

"Let's go over to Mo' Betta Burger, so we can call my mom, find out what happened with Def Duck Records, and go over our strategy."

"Um, I have to go buy new pointe shoes so I can start doubling up on my pointe work," I blurt out. "And then I have to go by American Ballet Th—"

"Yeah, but Melissa said she'll see you later. I'm not dumbo, gumbo, okay?" Bubbles says interrupting me. "That can wait."

"Oh," I say in a high voice, like I forgot. "Melissa is going to practice with me—you know, she's helping me out, because she goes to Ballet Hispanico."

"I know she goes to Ballet Hispanico," Galleria says, like, "Duh, duncehead, I'm at the head of the class, so don't try it." I don't think she likes the fact that Melissa is coming over.

"Um, we weren't going to practice today, were we?" I ask timidly. Suddenly, I feel my

75

throat getting tense. I feel overwhelmed, like my worlds are colliding, and I'm singing, dancing, and doing hair as fast as I can!

"I don't know. I have to see what Mom says," Galleria says strongly. "Maybe the Def Duck peeps will want a whiff of our riff right away, you know what I'm saying?"

I nod my head yes.

"You can go after we finish, can't you, Chuchie?"

"Um, *claro que sí*—of course," I back down, feeling totally embarrassed.

As we walk on Eighth Avenue to Mo' Betta Burger, Keisha Jackson from our homeroom class stops in our path. We're not feeling Keisha Jackson, and she's not feeling us, *está bien*? So we act like we don't see her, because we're so engrossed in our conversation. Actually, we're practically fighting. I can tell Bubbles doesn't like the idea of Melissa coming over to practice ballet with me. I guess she feels we should be spending every second outside of school doing something with the Cheetah Girls. But I want to practice ballet too. I just do!

"Yo, Galleria and Chanel," Keisha says. Galleria and I continue ignoring her, but

Dorinda sort of nods at her and says, "What's up, Keisha?"

"Yo, I was wondering if I could buy one of them Cheetah Girls chokers." Keisha holds her hands around her neck like she is choking herself.

I feel my cheeks burning. I can't believe she is still making fun of our Cheetah Girls chokers fiasco! See, when we first made them, and sold them to some peeps at school, they fell apart—the letters we glued on with Wacky Glue went kaflooey, and the snaps came off the closures in the back. I mean, it was *una tragedia*!

Bubbles stops in her tracks and looks straight at Keisha. Uh-oh—I'm getting that Showdown at the Okie-Dokie Corral feeling all over again. *Por favor, Dios, no otra vez!*

"Keisha," Bubbles says, getting that annoyed tone in her voice. "How are you gonna buy a Cheetah Girls choker from us when the word on the street is, 'You're as broke as a bottle.'"

"Ooooooo," two girls in Keisha's crew say in chorus.

"Well, I thought, since the letters keep coming off and the snaps don't snap, that maybe you were giving 'em away—you know, like they do when they're trying to get rid of damaged merchandise at the Home De-poooo."

"Oh, I see, Keisha, you're trying to show us that you do more than sleep in merchandising class. Wonder why you got a 'D' on the test then."

"How do you know what I got on the test?" Keisha asks, finally wiping the smirk off her face.

"I guess a little Red Snapper told me," Bubbles says, now satisfied that Derek Hambone was telling the truth after all. Everybody at school knows that Derek is cuckoo for Bubbles, so it doesn't take long for Keisha to figure out who the 'Red Snapper' is—since he's in her Merchandising class too.

"*Derek* told you?" Keisha asks, with enough attitude to hook a shark.

Bubbles ignores her again. Keisha finally struts away. Even though he can be a pain, I feel sorry for Derek now. I wouldn't want Keisha to be mad at *me*. She can breathe more fire than Puff the Magic Dragon—without even opening her mouth!

Once Keisha and her crew are on their way, Dorinda asks Bubbles, "When are we gonna sell some more Cheetah Girls chokers again, anyway?"

I feel my throat getting tense again. With

school, rehearsing for our group, practicing for the ballet audition, working at Toto in New York, Madrina's boutique—I don't want to think about one more thing! *No más, por favor!* I wait with bated breath for Bubbles' response.

"I think we'd better chill with the choker skills for now. I just want to get in with Mouse Almighty alrighty," Bubbles says, looking at us for support. "It makes me gaspitate to wait, you know what I'm saying?"

"Word. Me too," Dorinda says, hiking her cheetah backpack on her tiny shoulders, like her burden suddenly got heavier.

All of sudden, I trip on a crack in the sidewalk, and the sprain in my ankle starts to hurt again. "Ouch!" I wince.

"You all right, Chanel?" Dorinda asks, touching my arm.

"I hate the sidewalks here—the cracks are so big you could fall in a hole and nobody would find you for weeks." I don't want Dorinda to help me get my balance. I haven't told anybody that I've been feeling light-headed lately, and I don't want anybody asking me about it. I don't know why it's happening, but it just happened again, and that's kind of why I fell.

Whatever the reason, my ankle is bothering me again now. I limp a few steps to try and walk off the pain. I could whack Pucci for tripping me yesterday. That's probably why my ankle is still bothering me. Or maybe it's because I've been overdoing my ballet practice the last couple of days.

"Is your ankle still hurting, Chuchie?" Bubbles asks.

"No—I told you, it's fine now. I just slipped on the stupid rug that time!"

Dorinda and Bubbles look at each other like I'm getting cuckoo, which I'm not. I'm just tired of them making a big deal-io out of it. *Basta!*

Bubbles pulls out her cell phone to call *Madrina* at her boutique. While talking on the phone, she holds out her hand to Dorinda to do the Cheetah Girls' handshake. That means something good has happened. I get excited too—and then I feel suddenly nervous. What about my ballet practice?

We plop down at a bench in Mo' Betta's, and wait for Bubbles to get off the phone.

"We're in there like swimwear," Bubbles says, extending her hand to Dorinda to do the Cheetah Girls' handshake again.

Cuchifrita, Ballerina

Why didn't she do it to me? Suddenly, I feel jittery again.

"The Def Duck Records A&R guy on the East Coast—'member Freddy Fudge?—has agreed to let us do a showcase at the Leaping Frog Lounge downtown," Bubbles explains, chomping into her fries. "It seems they've got some new artists they want to check out, so Mom's idea was right on time."

"Why didn't they think of it themselves?" Dorinda asks, like she's our manager.

"I guess that's why *Mom's* our manager—so let's go with the flow!" Bubbles says, shrugging her shoulders. "They agreed with Mom, that maybe if Mouse Almighty sees us in action, he'll get the right honchos at the label to get on board our choo-choo train, and let him shop for some material for us—you know, look around for songs, I guess. He's got that kind of juice— that's what Freddy Fudge told Mom, anyway."

"Well then, what does Freddy Fudge do?" I ask.

"I guess buy suits and get his hair dyed daily," Bubbles chuckles. See, Freddy Fudge is this skinny guy with blond, short, fuzzy hair. When we went up to the record label to meet him and Mouse Almighty, Freddy was wearing this *tan coolio* black-and-white checked blazer with a red handkerchief in the pocket.

"He probably does like to shop a lot," I say to my crew.

"You would know—one shopaholic to another," Bubbles riffs.

I wish she would stop saying that about me. It's not exactly true. Well, not lately.

"I wish he would spend some time 'shopping' songs for us, so we could get in the studio and make a record," Dorinda says, huffing.

"So when do we get to be in this showcase?" I ask, feeling my heart fluttering. I hope it's not before my audition for the ballet company. Please don't let it be before my audition!

"They're gonna arrange it, and get back to Mom about it," Bubbles says. "It'll be good— once Mouse Almighty gets a whiff of our flavor, he's gonna want to shop for songs till he drops!"

"Word, let's hope so," Dorinda says, chomping on her burger like a mischievous chimpanzee. I don't want to tell her that she has ketchup on her mouth again, after all the time we've spent trying to teach her table manners. Meanwhile, I'm too nervous to eat, and Bubbles notices. "Chuchie, you're not gonna eat?"

"No—I have to go now and get my pointe shoes, and see if I got the audition appointment," I say nervously. I had an apple for breakfast and a glass of juice. I don't want to eat anything else today, because then I'll be too fat for my audition!

"You sure didn't eat a lot down in Texas—I was amazed," Bubbles says, trying to figure out what's going on.

Dorinda saves me from Bubbles interrogation when she blurts out, "What audition appointment?" I can't believe she's talking with her mouth full of Chunky Funky burger!

"Remember I told you on the plane?" I remind her. "I'm going to audition for the Junior Corps Division of the American Ballet Theatre—*if* I get the appointment, that is."

"Word?" Dorinda asks. Bubbles doesn't say a word. I know what they're both thinking— after that klutzy performance at the twins' house in Houston, the only thing I should be doing is pliés in my bedroom!

I give Dorinda a look, like, "We'll talk later." Sometimes Dorinda and I talk on the phone. I feel more comfortable telling her certain things than I do Bubbles. And sometimes Do' calls me, to tell me about what's going on in her house. She lives with her foster parents, Mr. and Mrs. Bosco, and ten foster brothers and sisters, and she has a lot of problems at home. I feel so bad for her sometimes. Even when Mom is being mean to me, I know that my Abuela Florita really loves me, and so does Princess Pamela, my dad's girlfriend. That's more than Dorinda has.

"Um . . . I gotta go," I say, feeling bad that I have to leave my crew.

"Okay—but we're definitely gonna start practicing Tuesday or Wednesday, so plan on it," Bubbles says in a mean tone.

"I know," I shoot back. "We can talk later in the chat room?"

Not looking up from her plate of french fries, Bubbles moans, "Whatever makes you clever."

Ever since we became the Cheetah Girls, she's starting to get a lot like Pucci—a real pain in the you-know-what!

Chapter 7

My heart starts fluttering as soon as I gaze into the window of the dance store, On Your Tippytoes. All those tutus, pointe shoes, and tiaras—*tan coolio*! I love dance shops—even the smell of new leather soles on ballet slippers makes me intoxicated!

Once inside, I head straight for the pointe shoes. On the way, I pass the rack for tights. I might as well pick up a new pair of pink ones for my audition, I tell myself. Pink tights and pink pointe shoes always make my legs look longer, and I want my legs to look like they go all the way to my neck!

While I try to find my size—petite—I hear someone in back of me mutter, "Excuse me."

"Oh, I'm sorry," I turn and apologize to this blond girl, because I'm blocking her view of the tights rack. As she reaches over me for a pair of flesh-colored tights, I notice that her hair is pulled back so tight that her eyes are slanting like a mummy's.

Yuk, why is she buying beige tights? I ask myself as she walks away. I look at her legs to see if she is a ballerina, but I don't think so. She must be a jazz dancer or something, because those tights are very, very unprofessional. I can just see Mrs. Bermudez, my old ballet teacher at Ballet Hispanico, pulling her to the side, and telling her so. "Pink is what dancers wear onstage," I heard her tell the *pobrecita* who made the mistake of wearing beige tights in class one day.

I scan the rack of pointe shoes—first picking up a pair of satin ones, then deciding on a pair of Capezios in leather. I ask the saleslady for a pair in a size seven. Taking off my red ballet flats and red socks, I wiggle my toes so they can breathe. That's when I notice that my big toe-nail is purple, and the rest of my toenails are an ugly yellow color. Oh, well, that's the price I have to pay for doing pointe work. I won't be getting a pedicure for a long time. When you're training, you need all the lumps, bumps, and calluses you can develop, to protect your tootsies.

The good thing is, I have a squarish foot with short toes that are almost all the same size. They are the best feet you can have as a ballerina. I didn't know this until Mrs. Bermudez looked at my feet one day and told me so. I'm also lucky because I don't have a high arch—which looks prettier in pointe shoes, but is not as strong or easy to control.

"How do those fit?" the saleslady asks me.

"Fine," I say, smiling as I gaze starstruck at my new Cinderella slippers.

"You look so pretty in that red outfit," the lady says, beaming at me. I wish I could tell her that she would look *tan coolio* in something red too, instead of that skirt suit in drab green—or as Bubbles would call it, "tacky khaki." Red would go better with her beautiful black hair and exotic brown eyes.

Just to make sure I don't insult her or something, I ask, "Where are you from?"

"Tokyo," she says, beaming at me like she's so happy I asked.

I'm not sure where Tokyo is. The saleslady

picks up on my blank expression and says, "Japan."

"Oh!" I exclaim, suddenly remembering that word the Japanese lady said at the Blessing of the Insects, when she tried to get past me to the altar. "Do you know what, um, 'cootie say' means?"

Suddenly I feel stupid. The saleslady is probably tired of people asking her questions like that, and making her feel like a foreigner all the time. (I know Mom hates it when people can tell she is Dominican. She likes to pretend that she is French, or even just plain ole American—which, according to my history teacher, Mr. Globee, doesn't even exist anyway.)

But it looks like the saleslady is getting more excited by my question than insulted, because she starts laughing. "Oh! Maybe you mean—*kudasai?*"

"Yes!" I say, so happy that we're finally speaking the same language.

"Yes—that means 'please' in Japanese!" she exclaims, and I can tell she is happy she could help me.

Now I stand on pointe to make sure their is enough room in the toe. Contrary to what people believe, the pointe shoe doesn't hold you up—it's your foot, supported by your legs, supported by your middle.

"I wish I could do that!" the saleslady exclaims.

I smile, but try not to get distracted by how nice she's being—because I have to concentrate to make sure these are the right shoes for me. Each and every pair of pointe shoes are hand-made, and they're kinda like snowflakes—they may look alike, but they're all unique, and have all sorts of variations in the sizing.

"Which company do you dance with?" the saleslady asks.

"Oh, I'm not with a company—yet," I say nonchalantly, but I'm so flattered that she thinks I am a professional ballerina. Now I feel as proud as a peacock—and my feathers are definitely starting to spread. "I have an audi-tion," I say. Then I realize that I'm telling a fib-eroni—because I don't even *know* yet if I have an audition — not until I leave here, and check with the American Ballet Theatre office.

Well, I *almost* have an audition. So I tell her, "I'm going to be doing 'Black Butterfly,' so I have to make sure the shoe is hard enough to do thirty-two *fouettes*." *Fouettes* are a very demanding type of turn, so I'll be *en pointe* constantly in front of the judges. Of course, I'm not going to have to do the whole piece for the audition—but still . . .

The saleslady is staring at me, waiting for me to make up my mind.

"I'll try one more pair before I decide," I tell her, hoping she doesn't get annoyed.

But I don't think she does, because she brings me three other kinds of pointe shoes, and lets me try them all on in peace.

"I'll take these," I tell the saleslady, finally deciding on the fourth pair, which seems to have the most room at the toe for padding. Once I get to the register, I ask for some ribbon and lambswool. The lambswool will protect my tootsies, and minimize the rubbing of the skin against my shoe, but still let me feel the floor.

"Which kind do you want?" the man behind the counter asks me, placing different types of lambswool on the counter so I can touch them.

"This one," I say, settling on the fluffier brand— which will wrap around my trouble spots (my big toe, the little toe, the knuckles, and the tips of my toes) without giving me grief afterward.

"How much ribbon do you want?"

Now is not the time to skimp on ribbon. "Um, six—no, make that six and a half yards," I say proudly. There has to be enough ribbon to cross over my foot at the front, and wrap twice around my ankle to tie in a neat knot (not a bow, which is very unprofessional) at the back, outside the ankle—the part that doesn't show when my feet are turned out.

"What color?" the man asks, annoyed because I'm holding him up, and he has other people to wait on. Everywhere you go in New York, there is always a line, it seems!

"Oh, I'm sorry—the flesh-colored one."

As I walk around the corner to the American Ballet Theatre, I stare closely at the sidewalk for any good omens. If I find money on the sidewalk—even a penny—in *brujería* it will mean something good is going to happen to me! Santa Maria, Sophia, and Catalina, please give me a sign—*por favor*!

Suddenly, I notice that I'm dillydallying on the sidewalk. I guess I'm nervous about going to American Ballet Theatre—what if they tell me I don't have an audition? Or that they lost my application? I'll die right there on the spot!

The Cheetah Girls

For the first time today, I wish Bubbles and Dorinda could be here with me. I always feel stronger when I'm around them. I smile to myself, thinking of the new nickname Bubbles gave me—Miss Cuchifrita Ballerina.

Oh, that's right. Aqua and Angie's school—the Performing Arts Annex—is right here in back of Lincoln Center too. Maybe I should try to find them? Nah—it's already four o'clock, and they've probably already left for the nearest BBQ hut. No, wait—there is one day of the week that they stay after school, and take extracurricular activities. Is it Monday or Thursday? I can't remember. I shake my head to get rid of the cobwebs—I suddenly feel so confused and light-headed.

At last, I find myself at the entrance of the American Ballet Theatre. Even though it's only three blocks away from the ballet shop, I feel like Little Red Riding Hood making her way through the forest! Taking a deep breath, I open the heavy wooden door. My heart is beating so fast when I walk up to the receptionist that I think I'm going to have a heart attack!

"Can I help you?" she asks, but she isn't smiling, which makes me even more nervous!

"I, um, filled out a form, I mean I sent in an application for the Junior Corps—"

"You want to know if you have an audition date?" the receptionist cuts me off.

"Um, *sí*—I mean, yes," I stutter. Now I'm really blushing, because I always lapse into Spanish when I'm nervous, and she must think I'm kinda slow or something!

"What is your name?"

"Chanel Simmons," I say quietly.

"Have a seat, someone will be right with you."

I always hate when people say that, because sometimes that means that you are in big trouble—like when I used to get called to the principal's office in grade school.

I look around at all the beautiful ballet posters in the office. Well, I am definitely not in grade school anymore. I'm sitting in the reception area of American Ballet Theatre—which has some of greatest ballet dancers in the world.

Ooo, look—Paulina Perez! I stare at the poster of one of my favorite ballet dancers. She is so beautiful and graceful. "There was never a more beautiful Giselle . . ."—that's what Mom said after she saw her in a production of it when she was younger.

"Chanel Simmons?" asks a lady who has stepped out from behind a door.

"Yes," I respond, snapping out of my daydream.

"Please, come in. I'm Mrs. Chavez, the Junior Corps registrar."

I follow her into a tiny, cramped office. "Please sit down," she says, motioning for me to sit in the chair directly opposite her desk. I wonder if this means I didn't get an audition.

Mrs. Chavez shuffles through some papers, then says, "Ah, yes." She sits quietly as she examines my form. I can tell it's mine, because I filled it out in red ink. Mrs. Chavez looks at me, but she isn't smiling. "I see you attended Ballet Hispanico from the age of six till twelve. Where did you go after that?"

"I, um, have been practicing at the studio in my, um, apartment, well, we live in a loft."

"Oh?"

"Um, we have a barre in the studio and everything. My mother takes, um, dancing," I say, deciding that I'm not going to tell Mrs. Chavez about Mom's latest obsession with wiggling her belly button in the mirror!

"Chanel—we received a recommendation from your teacher at Ballet Hispanico. She feels

Cuchifrita, Ballerina

you could do the work if you put your mind to it, but it seems—"

"I'm ready to put my mind to it now," I say, feeling the heat flash around my temples, then shut my *boca grande* out of embarrassment for interrupting Mrs. Chavez in the first place.

"Like I was saying," Mrs. Chavez says slowly, making me feel embarrassed all over again, "Mrs. Bermudez felt your decision to interrupt your studies was influenced by your best friend, um—?"

"Galleria."

"Yes," Mrs. Chavez says, then pauses, which I take as my cue to explain or plead my case.

"Galleria, um, didn't want to take ballet classes anymore—and even though I wanted to continue, I didn't. See, my parents were getting a divorce around that time, and I didn't want them to have to pay for it. . . ." I'm shrieking inside, because maybe I'm talking too much.

"The divorce?" Mrs. Chavez asks, confused.

"No!" I say, turning so red I match my sweater. "I mean, they didn't want to pay for my ballet classes."

"I see," Mrs. Chavez says, softening just a little—*gracias* gooseness! "Do you think you are really ready to dedicate your life to ballet?"

I freeze inside. What does she mean by *my life*? "Well, I'm ready to work really hard practicing and rehearsing." *Por favor, Dios*, please let that answer her question!

"I'm curious, Chanel—what made you change your mind?" Mrs. Chavez asks, and now I see a little twinkle in her eyes, which means she must like me.

"I'm fourteen now—and if I don't get into a company soon, it will be too late for me." I say, trying to seem as serious as I am.

"Dedicating one's life to ballet is a serious commitment—and very few girls each year are invited from outside the school to join the company in any of the divisions." Mrs. Chavez pauses again, as if she is thinking. "In light of Mrs. Bermudez's recommendation, we are going to allow you to audition for the Junior Corps."

"Thank you, Mrs. Chavez!" I say, finally letting out a sigh of relief.

"But I just want you to know, Chanel, that if you are not accepted, you may always feel free to audition for our school, or for other schools." Mrs. Chavez sounds like she's trying to soften the blow. "It's the pursuit of ballet that is most important—not the institution."

"But I want to be with American Ballet Theatre," I protest.

Before I can tell Mrs. Chavez why—because Paulina Perez is my favorite dancer in the whole world—she is dismissing me. "Here is the information you will need for the audition on Saturday."

Mrs. Chavez hands me a form, and I want to bolt for the door. *Corra, corra!* I should just run away now—I'm not ready for an audition yet!

Taking another deep breath, I realize that I'm as ready as I'll ever be. I have been practicing for weeks. Ever since October, when Dorinda auditioned to be a backup dancer for Mo' Money Monique's tour, I secretly knew I wanted to try out for ballet again, and I started to practice whenever I got the chance. I just never told anybody.

I only have to audition for fifteen minutes—what could possibly go wrong? I could do the steps from "Black Butterfly" backward—every combination, every *grande battement*, and, most importantly, every *fouette*—those beautiful turns that I have worked so hard to do perfectly.

Walking toward the subway, I read my audition sheet over and over, to make sure I don't miss anything. "Wear comfortable clothes. Don't do a segment longer than fifteen minutes. Blah, blah . . ."

I'm not looking where I'm going. As a result, I miss the first step going down to the subway, and almost trip down the rest! Luckily, the man in front of me breaks my fall.

"You all right?" he asks, concerned.

"Yes," I respond, feeling like a *babosa*. Whenever I get nervous, I always seem to do stupid things! I clutch the plastic bag containing my beautiful new pointe shoes. Catching my breath, I get to the bottom of the subway stairs in one piece. I can't wait to get home and sew on the ribbons, then break them in during practice with Melissa.

I chuckle, thinking about what Bubbles shouted out to Melissa this afternoon: "Melissa, don't dis her!" Bubbles is so funny. Suddenly, I feel a pang in my chest. I really do think of Bubbles as my sister. I wouldn't be here if it wasn't for her. I mean, going to Fashion Industries East High School and being in the Cheetah Girls.

Cuchifrita, Ballerina

The only thing we don't have in common anymore is ballet. I sigh away the sadness. If I could have one wish, I would ask a fairy godmother to make Bubbles a ballerina too—then we would really be the dynamic duo, bound till death—and we could pirouette to payday!

Chapter 8

I'm too excited to eat dinner. I run straight to the exercise studio, to sew the beautiful ribbons onto my pointe shoes. I plop down on the floor, happy that Mom and some lady I've never seen before are too busy in the den to care about me.

I rifle through my heart-shaped thread box, looking for the right thread to use. I put back the cotton thread, and settle on the crochet kind—it's stronger than cotton, which rots and snaps after being rubbed by my sweaty feet. I bend the heel so it lies flat against the side of my left pointe shoe. That way, I can find the right place to sew the ribbon.

After I finish, I sew dressmaker's tape on the

Cuchifrita, Ballerina

inside, to make the ribbons especially strong. This way, when I wear out these pointe shoes, I can use the ribbon over again. Sometimes I'm such a smart *señorita*! I say to myself proudly, as I sit and gaze at my pointe shoes. Then I change into my unitard and put them on.

The doorbell rings, and I jump up to get it, noticing that I'm feeling a little light-headed again. I wonder if I'm coming down with a virus, I think, panicking to myself. Maybe I'd better drink a glass of water.

"I'll get it," I yell, so Mom doesn't have to come out of the den. I want her to keep busy talking to the lady.

"*Hola*, Melissa!" I say excitedly, hugging her, then ushering her right into the exercise studio. Melissa is looking around like she is really impressed.

"Your hallway is five times bigger than my whole apartment!" she says with glee, then gasps at the exercise studio. "*Ay, Dios mío*, if I had this to practice in, I'd never leave my house!" Her eyes are moving around like pinballs.

"Well, I can't even get *in* here half the time," I protest. "My mother exercises twice a day."

"*Verdad?* Really?" Melissa asks, impressed.

"She used to be a model," I offer in explanation.

"Really?" Melissa says, sounding like a broken record.

"Really—and believe me, she works really hard to stay skinny. More than me!" I say, laughing. "Hey, guess what? I got an audition for the Junior Ballet Corps!!"

"Really?" Melissa responds, her big brown eyes opening even wider, but now even *she's* laughing at herself for saying the same thing over and over again.

"Really, *mija*—so we've got to practice hard!" I show off my new pointe shoes. "I went to Tippytoes after school."

"Well, let's break them in," Melissa says, getting serious. I can tell that she loves ballet as much as I do. She changes into her leotard and begins her warm-ups at the barre.

I can't help but notice how much smaller her butt is than mine. Suddenly, I feel insecure. *My butt sticks out too much for me to be a ballerina.*

"How is Mrs. Bermudez?" I ask. Now I miss her, since she gave me such a good recommendation to Mrs. Chavez.

"Strict as ever, but she doesn't teach the advanced classes anymore," Melissa says. "We have a new teacher, Mrs. Ferrer—she came from the Joffrey, and she's really strict."

"Really?" I respond, sounding just like Melissa. Joffrey Ballet School is in New York too, and it's just as famous as American Ballet Theatre. Maybe I should try out there, too. Their students graduate to the Joffrey Ballet Company, and to companies all over the world—sometimes even to faraway places like Eastern Europe, where Princess Pamela is from. That would be so exotic! I think dreamily to myself as I warm up.

Once we get into the meat of our ballet practice, Melissa and I aren't chatting anymore. You have to really concentrate on the *adagio* steps— preparations for turns that start out simple, but get a lot more difficult once you add the head and arm movements.

"Let's do *petit allegros* now, okay?" Melissa suggests.

I nod my head okay, and prepare for the small jumps—like the *changements* that come before the *grand allegros*—which call for bigger combinations on the diagonal. This is the stuff I have to be down on.

Now I start getting nervous, because it's time

to show Melissa what I'm gonna do for my audition. She does her cool-down—some *grand battements* and *ports de bras* with her arms—and watches me get ready to do my routine.

"Okay, *mija*—your extensions are good," Melissa says, smiling.

"I know," I say, touching my hair. "I just got them put in."

Melissa breaks out in a big smile at my joke. In ballet, an extension refers to how high you can lift your leg, in movements like the *battements* and *developpé*. I can lift my legs high, *está bien?*

Before I get too big-headed, Melissa barks, "Okay, now let's see your '*Mariposa Negra*.'" I've already told her I'm going to audition with a piece from the *Black Butterfly*, a famous Spanish ballet.

I take a deep breath and put on my audition music—it's by Tchaikovsky, the famous Russian composer of *Sleeping Beauty*, *Swan Lake*, and *Nutcracker* fame.

Melissa beams, and nods her head for me to begin. She sits on the floor like she is one of the judges, pretending she has pen and paper in front of her, and is writing notes on my performance.

Cuchifrita, Ballerina

I ignore her, because that's what you're supposed to do at an audition. You have to totally concentrate on every single step you take. I take a deep breath, and suddenly I'm feeling dizzy again. I shake my head for a second.

"*Qué pasa?*" Melissa asks, concerned.

"*Nada*—I feel dizzy, but I don't know why," I mutter, trying not to pay attention to the light-headedness.

"Have you eaten?" Melissa asks me.

"No," I respond, like, "what does that have to do with anything?" You never eat when you are rehearsing for a big performance—and this is a big performance, even if it is just an audition!

Melissa looks at me, but doesn't say anything. She nods her head again for me to begin. I start the Tchaikovsky tape, and put my hands over my head in *port de bras* position. Gingerly, I flutter my arms. I am playing one of the follower butterflies—to audition as the lead would have been too brazen, too conceited for a ballerina auditioning to get into Junior Corps Division.

I take a few steps *en pointe*—which is the easy part. It's going from flat to pointe, and coming down on one foot as well as two, that separates the *chicas* from the lead ballerinas, *entiendes*? I turn twice, then dip into a *fouette*, then turn again, maintaining my balance.

Ouch, my ankle hurts—and so does my head! I keep going—*jeté*, plié, *fouette*, and the leap that takes me halfway across the exercise studio—before I dive into a beautiful curtsy and drape my body to the floor.

"Bravo! Encore!" Melissa says, clapping loudly. I don't respond, because I cannot expect that at my audition. No one will clap. They will simply nod, and say "thank you"—and I will be expected to exit from the room immediately.

"Do I need any work?" I ask Melissa, wiping the sweat from my forehead with a hand towel.

"Yes," she responds without hesitating, and I feel the sting of rejection, even though I know she is being helpful. If there is anyone who wants me to do my best at this audition, it's definitely Melissa.

"Your *fouettes* feel forced. It looks like you don't have your balance when you come back to the center," Melissa instructs me.

"Okay," I moan, then put on the record and do the routine again. Melissa watches me carefully, and I try really hard to concentrate on my *fouettes*. I think it's because I feel dizzy that I don't quite get them. No, that isn't true—I *always* have trouble with them.

Melissa claps again when I finish, but this time she doesn't say "Bravo," or anything. I know it's stupid, but that makes me feel more nervous. Maybe I shouldn't even go to this stupid audition if I don't want to come off like a big *babosa*.

"I think you're ready," Melissa says with a sigh.

I take off my sweaty shoes and hang them over the barre, so they can dry and be ready for my big day on Saturday.

"Chanel!" I hear Mom yelling for me. Melissa and I hurry toward the kitchen. Mom is standing there with the phone in her hand. Funny, I didn't hear the phone ring. I guess I was really concentrating on my practice. I grab the receiver, and hear Bubbles's voice.

"*Mamacita*, we have a game plan," she coos. I guess she's trying to be nice to me, because she was so nasty when I wouldn't hang with her and Dorinda after school today.

"What happened?" I respond, waiting to hear the details.

"We have a showcase in two weeks—on a Friday night at seven o'clock," Bubbles says proudly.

"Really?" I respond, then catch myself, because I'm sounding like Melissa again. But I *am* surprised. I mean, *Madrina*—Bubbles's mom—can cook up things faster than Uncle Ben's Minute Rice, which is what Mom's cooking right now for dinner. (She always uses the white rice when we have company instead of the Goya yellow rice. I guess the lady with the big glasses is staying for dinner.)

"We're gonna rehearse starting Monday— you know, back to basics. We're just gonna give 'em 'Wanna-be Stars in the Jiggy Jungle,'" Bubbles explains, while I stand there in my leotard, feeling dirty.

"How come you're breathing so heavy?" Bubbles asks, finally noticing that I'm panting like a puppy.

"I, um, just finished doing my ballet practice—with Melissa," I explain nervously. Why should I feel bad? I guess I don't want Bubbles to think we're having fun without her.

"You're *still* practicing?" she asks, surprised. "It's nine o'clock already. I thought you said she was coming over at five o'clock!"

"She did," I protest. "Bubbles, the audition is Saturday. I have to be ready."

"That's good," Bubbles says like she means it—but even over the phone, I can tell when she is poking her mouth out and getting an attitude. "This way, you'll have it out of the way for our rehearsal."

I can't believe Bubbles! She's not even considering the possibility that I will get into the Junior Ballet Corps! I feel myself getting angry. Bubbles can write songs better than I can. Why can't she understand that I'm a better ballerina than she is? That's why I have to do this on my own—without her.

"If I get into the company, Bubbles, then I'm gonna have to rehearse—I'm just gonna somehow find time to do both. But for right now, it's fine."

"Well that's the point to this joint, Chuchie," Galleria says, in that big sister voice I hate. "If we do a showcase for the East Coast peeps at Def Duck Records, maybe they'll get us into the studio, and start wagging instead of lolly-gagging."

"I know. Don't worry, Bubbles, we're gonna rehearse really hard together, and be ready for all the quacking Ducks!"

Bubbles doesn't laugh at my joke. I guess she is *caliente* that I invited Melissa over to my house to practice with. I start feeling guilty, and then I get dizzy again. My legs feel weaker than a scarecrow's, and I plop right down at the dining room table. Melissa looks at me, concerned, and sits down too. Mom has come back from the den with the lady in the big glasses, so I don't want to stay on the phone.

"Bubbles, I feel dizzy. I'd better go—I have to shower and, um, *Mamí* has company, too."

"Mr. Tycoon?" Bubbles asks nosily.

"Um, no." I don't want to say anything about the lady, since she is hovering near the table. That would be rude. I know Bubbles is annoyed that I won't stay on the phone and talk with her, but I don't want to right now. "Bubbles, I have to leave at two o'clock to go to the audition. I'll call you afterward, *está bien?*"

"Okay," Bubbles says, giving in. "Good luck tomorrow." I think she means it.

Pucci comes into the dining room, and looks at Melissa out of the corner of his eyes. I introduce him, even though I don't want to. He mumbles a hello, then plops his Pick Up Stix game box on the table. Fumbling with a pile of Stix, he blurts out to Melissa, "Are you a Cheetah Girl too?"

"No," Melissa responds.

Cuchifrita, Ballerina

"Good," Pucci says, making a mischievous face.

"Pucci—get that box off the dinner table," Mom tells him, then introduces me to the lady in the big glasses. "This is Lois Paté—she is going to be working with me on my book."

"Hi, Ms. Paté," I say, noticing that her name rhymes with *plié*, which I don't want to think about until tomorrow morning when I get ready for my audition. Suddenly, I realize this is who Mom has been talking about on the phone—the "ghost writer"—but she doesn't look like a ghost to me. I wonder why they use that expression.

"I have to go," Melissa whispers to me. It is already getting late, and I know she has to travel all by herself on the subway to Washington Heights, which is in the upper part of Manhattan—almost all the way to the Bronx. I feel guilty that she has to go home by herself. I walk Melissa to the door, and she gives me a hug and says, "*Buena suerte* tomorrow. Good luck at the audition."

My hands are freezing; I'm so terrified. I run to my room and lie down without even taking a shower, because I am so dizzy I can't see straight. Plopping down on my bed, I pass out—just like Sleeping Beauty.

Chapter 9

I thought I knew what it meant to be scared, but now I know what terror really is. Just the thought of seeing Mrs. Chavez and the other judges watching me at the audition is enough to send me running for the hills. Still, I am so proud of myself—because even though my stomach was growling this morning, I didn't eat anything, and now I don't feel hungry at all. I feel like I'm floating on air.

When I open the door of the American Ballet Theatre, I stand as tall as I possibly can, like I'm not nervous about anything. *Nada, está bien?* I'm going to leap into stardom, that's what I'm going to do!

Then that stupid little voice comes into my

head again. *Maybe the judges won't think I'm so good.* I start shaking as I sit down in the waiting room.

A lady with a sharp voice instructs me to change in the anteroom studio. *This is it.* Now I will know if I have what it takes to be a ballerina—or not.

I turn nervously and look at the other girl in the anteroom, who has already changed. She looks a little older than I am, and she has long black straight hair pulled back into a ponytail. I watch her as she stands and does pliés— warming up and getting ready for the big time. Then she walks over to her canvas bag to get something out. I sneak a glance at her butt. She doesn't have one at all! I start shrieking inside again. How could I be so flat-chested, yet have a butt that sticks out?

"Chanel Simmons?" says a lady, sticking her head around the door. She is holding a clipboard. I wonder how I got called before the other girl. She must be early, I guess.

"Do you have a tape?" the lady asks me.

I hand her my Tchaikovsky cassette, which is clearly marked "Blank" on Side Two, so the assistant won't have any trouble figuring it out.

I sneak one last look at myself in the mirror as I walk to the center of the exercise studio. My hair is slicked up in a ponytail, and the styling gel is holding up okay, because I don't see any frizzies trying to take over.

Standing in the center of the studio, trying not to look at the judges, I feel the strangest feeling in my life—it's as if I have left my body, and I'm watching myself from above, where I'm floating. Suddenly, I feel my hands shaking, and I hope no one notices it but me. All that matters now is, it's time to dance!

The music has begun, and I begin to do the movements from the *"Mariposa Negra"* ballet piece. I place my hands over my head in *port de bras* position and my feet in fifth—then begin my pliés and *petit allegros* before I do my first *fouette.*

All of a sudden, I feel like I'm going to faint! Not now, *Dios*, please! I pray, as I do another *fouette*, then get ready for my series of grand leaps. One, two, three—

I leap, then turn—but lose my balance instead! "Aaah!" I scream, as I fall backward onto the floor—and disappear into darkness!

When I wake up, I see Mrs. Chavez and one of

the other judges huddling over me. *Ay, Dios mío*—I must have blacked out! I feel a sinking feeling in my stomach, and then—worse—a shooting pain in my left ankle.

"Drink this," Mrs. Chavez instructs me, handing me a paper cup of water.

"I don't know what happened!" I moan, now that I am conscious and fully aware of my *catástrofe*.

I ruined my audition! Tears start streaming down my face. My left ankle feels like it's on fire!

"You, um, fell and passed out," Mrs. Chavez says, waiting patiently for me to stop moaning. "Drink this water, please."

A lady comes with a wet washcloth and puts it over my forehead. "EMS is coming. They're going to take you to the hospital," she says.

"Hospital? I don't need to go to any hospital," I say, trying to talk normally between grimaces.

"Can you move?" Mrs. Chavez asks me.

I try to lift myself up without putting any weight on my left foot—but as soon as I get midway off the ground, I feel a shooting pain in my butt.

"Mr. Herrera, we'd better put her in the wheelchair," Mrs. Chavez says.

"We're gonna lift you up, Chanel," Mr. Herrera informs me. "Hector, can you come here, please?"

I don't want to be lifted up—I want to walk, but I'm too scared to try. Mr. Herrera and Hector get on each side of me and pick me up.

"Oouch!" I scream. My left ankle, dangling in midair, burns.

"Just one more second, Chanel. Can you sit like this in the wheelchair?"

"NO!" I cry out.

"Okay, then, we'll wait for the stretcher," Mr. Herrera says, as they put me back down on an outstretched blanket.

When the ambulance people arrive, Mrs. Chavez instructs them, "She's gonna need a stretcher."

I feel like such a *babosa*. What happened? I don't remember! Suddenly everything just went blank. . . . I guess the dizzy spells were an omen that something bad was gonna happen. I should have listened!

"I'm sorry I ruined your auditions," I say to Mrs. Chavez earnestly.

"That's okay, Chanel, we'll be fine," she says, and I notice the tiny furrows in her forehead get deeper. She is probably worried that they'll get in trouble or something.

The ambulance people return with a stretcher. "Okay, one, two, three." I feel the shooting pain in my butt as they pick me up, but I try not to yelp anymore.

"Where does it hurt?" asks one of the ambulance attendants.

"In my, um, near my backside, and my left ankle," I explain, trying to be mature.

Inside the ambulance, an attendant puts an oxygen mask over my face. I start to panic. What if I don't wake up? Fresh, hot tears roll down my cheeks. Not waking up would be better than living through this!

The attendant takes a tissue and wipes my face, then secures the oxygen mask, covering my nose. I close my eyes, and listen to the whirring sound of the siren. This is the first time I've ever been in an ambulance.

Suddenly I see Abuela's face before my eyes. She had to be taken to the hospital once, when she fell on the icy sidewalk in her neighborhood. Abuela is going to be so disappointed in me, I think, breathing in the oxygen and drifting off to sleep.

The Cheetah Girls

As I'm carted into the Lincoln Hospital Emergency Room, I try to decide who I would least want to see now—Mom, Abuela, or Bubbles. When I wake up and see Mom's face, I finally decide—it's Mom.

The attendant wheels me into a small room with a white curtain. "A nurse will be with you shortly," he says, and leaves. Mom stands next to me until another attendant comes in, and gives me a paper gown to put on. Mom tries to help me get out of my leotard.

"I can't," I scream. The attendant gets some scissors, and starts to cut off my leotard! Tears are streaming down my face.

"Don't cut my shoes!" I beg.

"We won't have to if we can get them off," he replies.

Mom hurriedly unties my pointe shoes. I know she doesn't want to waste the fifty dollars. "No duckets down the bucket," as Bubbles would say. Now I wish Bubbles was here to comfort me.

"Did you call Bubbles?" I ask Mom. I'm happy to see that the rash on her face is clearing up. Still, when I look at her, I see this image of her wearing that scary hockey mask.

Cuchifrita, Ballerina

"Don't worry about Bubbles now, okay?" Mom says sternly.

My ankle feels like a football. The attendant takes my pointe shoes and cut leotard, and puts them in a paper bag, then staples it closed. "You can get these when she's being released."

"Thank you," Mom tells him.

After the attendant leaves, we sit there in silence. I'm so relieved that Mom doesn't say anything to me while we're waiting for a nurse, doctor, or the Boogie Man to come see me. *Please, somebody come!* I lie there, resigned, with my eyes closed. The throbbing pain doesn't matter anymore. Nothing matters now, because I didn't get into the Junior Corps, and I'll be lucky if anybody ever lets me audition again!

Gracias gooseness, a nurse comes right in and starts poking around. "We have to take some blood samples," she says nicely. "And if you could fill out these forms—and make sure to include your insurance card."

Mom takes the clipboard and starts scribbling stuff.

The nurse takes out the needle and sticks me in the arm. I keep my eyes closed real tight.

Even though I hate needles, I'm not going to show Mom that I'm afraid.

While we're waiting for the doctor to come into the room, I watch the solution dripping into my IV bottle. It puts me into a trance. It seems like a thousand years before the doctor finally comes into the little room to see me.

"Hi, I'm Dr. Reuben," she says, looking at me curtly, then checking the chart at the foot of my bed. "Okay, I see we have swelling in your left ankle. Let me examine it. I'm going to touch your leg and ankle, Chanel, to determine the range of motion. You tell me where it hurts."

Every way the doctor touches, I scream, "Ouch!!!"

"We're going to have to take X rays now, to see if her ankle is broken. Mrs.—"

"Simmons," Mom says.

The doctor then turns me over on my stomach, with the help of the nurse.

"Tell me where it hurts," Dr. Reuben says, moving her hands on different parts of my back.

"Lower," I instruct her. "Ouch!!" I wince, when she touches the top of my backside.

When Dr. Reuben finishes, the nurse informs

Mom, "Just have a seat and wait here until we come back."

Mom sits in a chair, and doesn't even look at me while I'm being wheeled out to the X-ray room. But when I get back, there is a flicker of warmth in Mom's eyes like she is happy to see me.

After the attendant leaves, I moan to Mom, "I didn't do so well at the audition."

"What happened. *Qué pasó?*"

"I don't know," I stutter, then start crying again, which makes me feel so stupid!

After that, Mom doesn't say a word, and I'm staring at the ceiling. It seems like a thousand more years before Doctor Reuben comes back in.

"Okay. From your X rays, Chanel, it looks like you have a broken tailbone and a Grade II ankle sprain in your left ankle. Have you sprained your ankle before?" Dr. Reuben asks me, shoving her hands in the pocket of her lab coat.

"Um, yes—last week, in Houston," I confess. Mom looks at me surprised. "But, it was just a little sprain. Nothing like this."

"That's probably why there is so much inflammation and purple shading," Dr. Reuben continues. "Well, it's going to take six months or longer to heal completely."

"Six months!" I say, squeaking. *Bubbles is gonna kill me!* What about our showcase?

"But, it will improve tremendously after a three- to four-week healing period," Dr. Reuben adds, upon seeing the alarmed look on my face.

"Am I going to be able to dance again?" I ask.

"Once an ankle sprain occurs, the joint itself may never be as strong as it was before the injury. But you'll regain strength in time," Dr. Reuben says. She is a very serious lady, so I can't tell if she is just being nice and trying not to scare me. "Are you a dancer?"

"Yes," I say, and it's hard to believe my own ears. "But not a professional one."

"Well, if all goes well, you'll be able to bear full weight on your ankle within a four-week healing period," Dr. Reuben continues. "The initial treatment is what I call RICE—Rest, Ice, Compression, and Elevation."

I sink into the bed, feeling hopeless. I don't want any RICE treatment!

"You're going to have to apply ice packs to the sprained ankle for thirty-minute periods, every three to four hours," Dr. Reuben tells Mom. "You should also apply compression with an elastic wrap, but don't wrap it so tightly that her circulation is blocked. And while she's resting, elevate the ankle by propping up the leg with pillows."

"What about the tailbone?" I ask, wondering what concoctions Dr. Reuben has for that.

"Oh, there's not much you can do for that. The tailbone is very delicate, and it heals itself naturally. Just put on ice packs and some arnica—rub it on like a balm."

"How long does she have to stay here?" Mom asks.

"She can leave now. She'll be much more comfortable at home. There's no need to keep her here," Dr. Reuben says assuredly.

I don't wanna go home! I want to shriek to Dr. Reuben, but I don't say anything.

"Here are your crutches. You should use them until you can walk without pain," Dr. Reuben says, instructing the nurse to place the crutches near me by the bed.

"Don't you have to wrap her ankle?" Mom asks. I guess she doesn't want the doctor to think she means my tailbone.

How am I going to tell my crew that I broke my tailbone at the audition? I would rather have suffered a head concussion!

"No, Mrs. Simmons. After a few weeks, we're gonna put a brace on it if it doesn't heal properly. It should, though, if she completely stays off it for the first week."

One week in prison. That's all I can think of.

"One more thing," the doctor says, her face growing more serious. "About the dizzy spells you were having? Chanel, have you been going without eating?"

"I . . . well, I . . ." She can tell I have, and so can Mom, who looks at me in horror, her eyes wide. "I didn't want my butt sticking out at the audition. . . ." I say meekly, sounding lame even to myself.

"Chanel, have you ever heard of anorexia?" the doctor asks. When I don't answer, she says, "It's when people starve themselves because they think they're too fat. Now, you are definitely in the normal weight range. You do not need to diet, and you certainly shouldn't be starving yourself. That's why you passed out—and if you'd kept it up much longer, you could have done serious long-term damage to yourself."

"Really?" I say, in a voice so meek it's almost a whisper.

124

"Really. People die of anorexia, Chanel. Young girls die. Now you've got to get your strength back up. I suggest you eat whenever you're hungry, as long as it's healthy food."

"Yes, ma'am," I say. "I mean, yes, Doctor."

As I am being wheeled out of the emergency room and into a fancy van, all I can think about is what a stupid *babosa* I've been. If I hadn't been so concerned about my butt that I stopped eating, it wouldn't be broken right now. Maybe I'd even be in American Ballet Theatre Junior Corps Division! And my ankle wouldn't look like a purple grapefruit. When that doctor said I could have died, I got really scared, and I'm still shaking as Mom wheels me outside, where a big, fancy van is waiting for us.

"Kashmir arranged for the van," Mom explains to me. I wince. It figures that Mom called Mr. Tycoon for help, and not Daddy.

That's okay. I'm going to call Daddy myself when I get home.

As soon as I'm all propped up in my bed, Bubbles calls—before I get a chance to call Daddy. Mom takes the phone from me, and tells Bubbles to call back tomorrow. I'm so relieved. I know Bubbles will be upset with me

125

when she finds out we won't be able to do our showcase in two weeks for Def Duck Records.

"You can come by tomorrow," Mom explains sternly to Bubbles.

For once I am happy that Mom is related to Puff the Magic Dragon. Nobody can breathe more fire than her—except maybe *Madrina*, Bubbles's mom. . . .

I don't know what time it is when I wake up, but the sun is shining through my bedroom window. I look down, and see that I'm wearing my pink flowered nightgown. Now I remember Mom putting it on me, but that's the last thing I remember. I look over at my alarm clock—the neon numbers say it's 9:00 A.M.

Nine o'clock in the morning! Why didn't anybody wake me up?! Suddenly, when I feel the shooting pain in my lower back, I remember why—because I'm not going to school today.

I can't believe I slept the whole night without waking up! Shaking my head some more, I realize that today is Sunday. There's no school anyway.

Then I smell something cooking in the kitchen, and notice that my stomach is growling really loud.

"Mamí!" I yell.

Pucci peeks his head in the door. *"Mamí* wants to know if you're hungry."

"Yes!" I exclaim. He runs out, without even saying anything nasty. I feel really weak—like I haven't eaten for a thousand years.

Mom comes into the bedroom with breakfast on a tray. I can't remember the last time she did that! "Don't tell me you're not going to eat anything again," Mom huffs. "Remember what that doctor told you."

"Don't worry," I say, biting off a sausage. "I'm going to eat everything on this plate. I've never been so hungry in my whole life!"

"Galleria and her mother are coming over at ten o'clock. After you finish eating, I can bring a pan and some water to give you a sponge bath," Mom says.

"A sponge bath?" I squeal. "I can—" I stop myself, because I realize that I can't, so I just sigh and say, "Okay."

Four sausages, two English muffins, and four scrambled eggs later, Mom gives me a sponge bath, which makes me feel like a little girl again. I feel so humiliated, but I don't want to start crying again.

"I'm going to get better real quick," I say to Mom. She doesn't say anything—not even "I told you so." She didn't want me to try out for the Junior Corps, because she knew I wasn't ready. That's probably why I got so nervous and ruined everything. I feel so stupid now—I probably dieted myself right out of a place in American Ballet Theatre's Junior Corps Division!

"Which nightgown do you want to wear?" Mom asks me.

"The cheetah one," I say with a sigh. If my friends are coming over, I want to let them know I'm still a Cheetah Girl—even if this cheetah is a hurting kitty.

Mom brings in a bucket of ice, to do the ice packs on my ankle and tailbone.

"It's so cold," I say, shivering. "I can't believe I have to do this fifty times a day!"

"You're lucky your ankle isn't broken," is all Mom says, but I know she wants to say more.

Luckily, the doorbell brings. I motion to Mom for her to hurry up.

"Don't worry," she says. "I'm sure they've seen ice packs before!"

For once, I keep my *boca grande* shut. Pucci

opens the door, and I hear everyone talking in the hallway.

"In here!" Mom yells, but Pucci is already bringing them into my bedroom. He comes in first, and stands at the edge of my bed with his box of Pick Up Stix.

Madrina looks even taller than usual. With her big Cheetah hat on her head and high heels, she almost touches the ceiling!

"Chanel, you look swell," *Madrina* says, bending over to kiss me. "We brought you something from all of us."

Bubbles comes from behind her, and puts a big box with a big cheetah bow on top of me on the bed.

"Ooooo!" I coo. "What is this?"

"Open it and you'll see," Pucci says, like a smarty-pants.

"He's right, darling," *Madrina* says, sitting on the edge of my bed. "You won't know unless you open it."

Then I see that the rest of the Cheetah Girls are here, too. "Hi, Do' Re Mi!" I exclaim, as Dorinda comes into the room and bends over to kiss me. "Hi, Aqua. Hi, Angie!" The twins come over and kiss me, too.

The Cheetah Girls

"Does it hurt?" Bubbles asks.

"Yeah."

"Lemme put some more pillows under your head," Mom says, propping me up some more.

"*Gracias, Mamí*," I say, intent on unwrapping the bow on the big, beautiful box. "Aaah!" I exclaim when I see the layers of cheetah tissue paper inside.

Inside the box is a tutu covered with cheetah ribbons! "Ooo, this is *tan coolio*," I say, tears coming to my eyes. "Where did you find this?"

"It's just a tutu," Madrina explains.

"Bubbles and I sewed on the ribbons," Dorinda says, chuckling. "Look underneath, too."

"Oh!" I say, realizing there is more. Under more tissue paper, there is a cheetah leotard! "Ooo!"

"We thought if you want to be a cheetah ballerina—maybe sometimes when we do our shows, you could do ballet moves or something," Dorinda explains carefully.

The tears overflow from my eyes. And I thought my crew would be so mad at me!

"Chuchie, I think that would be sort of cheetah-licious. You know, as usual, the Cheetah Girls are coming with their own flavor. Miss Cuchifrita Ballerina isn't gonna sleep on her leaps," Bubbles says proudly.

"I think it would be dope—you know, we could be leaping at the Leaping Frog," Dorinda explains earnestly.

"But we're not going to be able to do the showcase in two weeks," I say sadly.

"I know." Bubbles sighs, then turns to leave.

"Where ya going?" Pucci asks her.

"I wanna get some Dominican punch—I know Auntie Juanita has made some," Bubbles jokes. Mom's idea of Dominican punch is mixing tropical punch with diet orange soda and root beer. I think it tastes yucky, but Bubbles likes it.

"I'll get it," Pucci volunteers, surprising us all.

"Get me one too, Pucci darling," *Madrina* coos proudly at Pucci. Then she takes my hand and says assuringly, "Don't worry, Chanel. I called Freddy Fudge at Def Duck Records, and told him to push the showcase back by another week. God knows they've done enough quacking about nothing, so one more week isn't going to make a difference in that little pond."

"They're still panting like puppies, don't you worry!" Aqua pipes up, then opens up her Cheetah backpack, and pulls out our Miss

Sassy trophy! "We think you should keep Miss Sassy for a while."

I start boohooing some more. "Thank you. She'll be very happy here. I'm going to put her right next to Mr. Smoochy-Poochy Hugs and Kisses," I coo, pointing to my stuffed dog on the shelf.

"I thought his name was Snuggly Wiggly?" Bubbles says smirking.

"I'm still dizzy, *mija*."

Everybody smiles at me. I feel so much better, now that I know they care about me.

"If we do the Def Duck showcase in three weeks, do you think they still wanna do it at the Leaping Frog?" I ask *Madrina*, squinching up my nose.

"Why? You don't want it there?" *Madrina* asks, ever the manager.

"Well, if it's okay with you, I would rather not hear the word 'leaping' for a while."

Angie, Aqua, Bubbles, and Dorinda start giggling. "Leapin' lizards, why on earth not?" Aqua asks.

"Because—I don't think I'll be leaping into stardom anytime soon, okay?" I say, giggling.

"No?" Bubbles asks, not believing her ears.

Cuchifrita, Ballerina

"No," I say, smiling and wiping away my tears. "No pirouettes till payday!"

Bubbles kisses me on the cheeks and says, "Now that's a song, Miss Cuchifrita Ballerina!!!"

Miss Cuchifrita, Ballerina!

Chanel's so swell
'cuz she's got the moves
Plié, sashay
Pirouette till payday!

Plié, sashay
Pirouette 'till hey day.
That's what we say
So don't shout né né
Hey,
Ho,
Go with the flow
And act like you know!

The Cheetah Girls Glossary

Adagio: In Italian it means slow; in ballet class, it refers to slow, stretchy exercises at the barre or in the center which have to do with balance, extension, and long lines in the body.

Allegro: The part of the ballet class when you learn small jumps.

Attitude: Working a situation. In ballet, it's a position in which the working leg is bent, not straight, and may be raised to the front, the side, or the back.

Babosa: Spanish for cuckoo head; idiot.

Barre: The barre is the wooden or metal railing that is either attached to the wall of the classroom or exercise studio, or moved to the center and used as a support. You rest your hand gently on it and don't clutch it for dear life!

Cáyate la boca: Spanish for "Shut your trap!"

Claro que sí!: Spanish for "Of course, you silly nilly."

Clunkheads: Dodo birds. Dunces.

Copyright infringement: When you bite someone else's flavor—like their music or lyrics—and act like it's your own—without giving them credit or duckets.

Corra, corra!: Run like a hyena!

Ding, ding: Exactly, duncehead.

Down in the Dumpster: Sad.

Gracias gooseness: Thank goodness.

Grand allegro: The large, diagonal combination at the end of ballet class where the jumps get more "grand," or bigger.

Extension: Hair weave; in ballet, it refers to how high you can lift your leg in movements like *battements* and *developpé*.

Howdy do: A common greeting in Houston that really means, "Wazzup?"

La culpa mía: Spanish for "my fault" or "my boo-boo."

Mackin': Sweatin' or swooning for someone or even daydreamin' about them all the time.

Mariposa negra: Black Butterfly.

Párate!: Spanish for "Stop, you cuckoo bird!"

Perpetrate: To do something shady or pretend that you're something you aren't.

Petit allegro: Any jump in ballet from one leg to another.

Pirouette till payday: Dancing till the duckets fall from the sky.

Pliés: Deep knee bends as performed in ballet warm-up exercises.

Port de bras: How you move your arms in different positions in ballet class.

Silly mono: Silly monkey. As in, "Stop acting like a silly *mono*!"

Terminado: Spanish for "finished." Kaput.

Tight: Dope. Brilliant.

Youston: The way some peeps down south pronounce "Houston."

ABOUT THE AUTHOR

Deborah Gregory earned her growl power as a diva-about-town contributing writer for ESSENCE, VIBE, and MORE magazines. She has showed her spots on several talk shows, including OPRAH, RICKI LAKE, and MAURY POVICH. She lives in New York City with her pooch, Cappuccino, who is featured as the Cheetah Girls' mascot, Toto.

 JUMP AT THE SUN

Hey, Girlfriend!

Would you like to be a member of our club?

Just for me! by PRO-LINE

VIP CLUB

Black History Profiles
Internet Safety
VIP Parties

Join Today!

Become a Just for Me VIP Member and get the official club membership kit today!
The membership kit includes a Just for Me VIP Club: Membership Card, Newsletter, Do Not Disturb Door Hanger, Passport to Fun, Scrungies, Bookmark, Coupons, ID Fingerprint Card, and Membership Flyer. In addition, you will receive a birthday card, a birthday surprise, and bimonthly newsletters.
Official Enrollment Form: Make sure you fill this form out completely. Print clearly. We cannot be responsible for lost, late, misdirected, or illegible mail. Enclose $9.95 plus one Just for Me proof of purchase (front panel), for membership in the JFM VIP Club, or $19.95 with no proof of purchase. Make check or money order (no cash) payable to: Just for Me VIP Club c/o Pro-Line Corp., P.O. Box 222057, Dallas, Texas 75222-9831

Name: _____ Date of Birth: _____

Address: _____

City: _____ State: _____ ZIP: _____

Day Phone: _____ Evening Phone: _____

Parent signature: _____

ail membership forms to: **Pro-Line Corporation   Attn: JFM VIP Club Membership   P.O. Box 222057   Dallas, TX 75222-9831**